DEATH IN THE NIGHT

The Soldier of Death walked quietly behind the nun, falling back into the shadows, remaining out of sight. The Soldier of Death followed her, never losing sight of her habit, bobbing up and down in front of him. He had come for her. By his hand, she must die. It was the only way. He was the Chosen One and she was just another one of the Intended. He picked up his pace as the sister cut across Bughouse Square. She was passing in front of the Newberry Library. The Soldier of Death held his breath as he fell into step right behind her.

Sister Fitzgerald came to the edge of the park and stepped out of the lights and into the dark shadows of the street. The Soldier saw his opportunity and pounced. He grabbed the petite woman from behind, covering her mouth with his gloved hand, his other arm locked around her waist. She didn't have a chance to scream. He dragged her down the street about half a block, her legs flailing, thrashing out at the empty air.

The alley was only a half block from the park and was dark and quiet. . . .

FOR THE DEFENDANT

E. G. SCHRADER

LEISURE BOOKS NEW YORK CITY

*To my husband and parents, who taught me the art of
perseverance and how not to let go; and to Kendall and Casey,
who showed me dreams do come true. And in remembrance of the
many who have lost their lives or families to religious violence.*

A LEISURE BOOK®

July 2004

Published by

Dorchester Publishing Co., Inc.
200 Madison Avenue
New York, NY 10016

ISBN 0-8439-5373-X

The name "Leisure Books" and the stylized "L" with design are
trademarks of Dorchester Publishing Co., Inc.

Printed in the United States of America.

Visit us on the web at www.dorchesterpub.com.

FOR THE DEFENDANT

Prologue

The boy heard a small tap on the door before his mother peeked her head into his room.

"Have you said your prayers, Hail Mary, Our Father?"

His little hands clasped tighter and beads of sweat dampened his forehead.

"Yes, Mother."

"All one hundred of them? Don't lie to me. And you know you can't lie to God. He'll know if you're lying or not."

His knees hurt from kneeling on the carpetless floor.

"I'm almost through."

"You need to ask for forgiveness and cleanse your soul. Or you're bound to end up just like your rotten father."

His stomach growled as it did most every night from being sent to bed without the luxury of a meal.

"Yes, Mother," the boy mumbled, secretly wonder-

1

ing what his father had done to make his mother hate him and say such vile things.

She closed the door and he heard the key in the lock, listening for the metal bolt to turn.

Click.

And he was alone.

The room was pitch black but for a sliver of light shining through a small chip he had scratched off in the dark paint that covered the windowpane. He crept into his bed and stared up at his ceiling. If he closed his eyes tightly, when he reopened them, he could see brilliant spots all over the ceiling. After opening his eyes, he would count the moving spots as they darted around the room. He methodically closed and opened, closed and opened his eyes, over and over again. The boy followed this ritual nightly, blocking out the noises from the streets below. Blocking out the sound of other children playing.

More importantly, the boy concentrated very hard on the bright spots before they faded from his vision to block out the monsters. He would pray each night that the monsters would not come back, but every night they came to him, voices haunting and tormenting him in the dark.

He would open his eyes quickly, staring at the closet door, waiting for someone or something to appear. He would leap from his bed, hoping to avoid an errant hand or tentacle grabbing at him, trying to pull him below the bed. He would lash out with his arms at the air above him, chasing away any lingering spirits. But there were never any ghosts. No monsters leapt from the closet, and no hand pulled him beneath the bed.

There was just him and his tormented mind, racing and tunneling through the lonely nights, holding on for the next morning, patiently awaiting the sound of the bolt turning.

Click.

And the door would open for him.

He would eagerly race to school in the morning, savoring every moment of sunshine and dreading the night to follow. Dreading the monsters and the voices, not realizing that there was just him, alone, in the dark.

Book One

The Good Doctor

Chapter One

Cook County Detention Center
Chicago, Illinois
October 2
10:43 A.M.

James rocked back and forth in his cell, trying to keep the cold air from gripping his body. Built in 1929 directly behind the courthouse, the Division 1 jailhouse reminded most people of a European dungeon. Its thick stone walls looked bleak on even the brightest of summer days. The steel bars separating each man from his freedom were ancient, not even used in modern jail construction. The worst of it was the cold that funneled its way through the aisles, moving through the building, enveloping every prisoner and guard. The

7

wind churned through the cell house, chilling it on even the warmest of fall days.

This particular morning was unusually cold for October, even in Chicago. A front had come down from the north, creeping in off Lake Michigan. With the wind whipping past his cell, James rocked harder, listening to the incessant water dripping from the faucet into the tiny sink in the corner.

James had been in Block Three, Cell 42, Division I of the Cook County Detention Center for what seemed like eternity. By actual count, it only amounted to a few months. Not that it mattered. Time was one thing James had plenty of, and thus far, Division I had done a remarkable job of taking it from him.

Division I was the oldest and dreariest of the buildings on the sprawling Cook County Jail campus. The county basically dealt with it as if it were an unsightly sore on the face of their city, which meant they tried to pretend it wasn't there.

The other buildings were much newer, modernized, and housed some of the more dangerous criminals. On the other side of the campus Division XI, a maximum-security building and one of the more recently built, housed the witness protection folks, as well as the criminals, if one could distinguish between the two. Division XI was a world away from its older counterpart. Not that either were luxury residences, but the differences were more than notable.

Division I held the politically powerless, the immigrants, the forgotten, the weak and the condemned.

Once relegated there, no one cared about them. Not even God.

James, unfortunately, was a nobody. Nobody dangerous, nobody notorious, nobody connected. Just plain nobody. A Jamaican immigrant, James had resigned himself to the fact that he was as much a part of Division I by now as it was of him.

James picked up his head when he heard one of the guards walking down the cell aisle. He continued rocking back and forth, listening to the sound of the guard's boots on the concrete floor. They stopped a few feet away from his cell.

"Hey, can I get something for my arthritis? The cold is making it ache so bad. I need to go see the nurse," an inmate begged.

The guard wasn't biting. "You can fill out a medical request if you want. Someone will be around soon. You're not leaving your cell, though. Sorry."

The noise from the guard's shoes dwindled as he walked back down the aisle, slipping out of James's hearing range.

"Psst. Hey, Judge."

There was no response.

"Hey, Judge," James whispered a little louder.

Judge was one of the older detainees. He had been in and out of prison and pushed through the system so many times he could map out the criminal justice process on the palm of his hand. Everyone called him Judge because he knew the judges in the building so well, he could tell an inmate what he'd be offered before he went into court. He could also tell you whether the judge would be pro-State or pro-defendant.

"Yeah, Spiritboy, what you calling me for?" Judge finally answered.

"My case is up tomorrow. I want to ask you about it."

"Oh yeah?"

"Mmhmm," James mumbled.

"All that praying and chanting you're always doing should help you out, no?" The older man chuckled.

"Maybe it might take a little more, I'm thinking," James replied.

The other detainees knew James for his Rastafarian beliefs, and jokingly referred to him as Spiritman, Spiritboy, or sometimes Rasta James, depending on who was talking to him.

"Heads up," Judge called out. "We got something coming your way."

Judge passed a folded note through his bars to his neighbor, the usual method of communication in the jail, coded notes or other signals.

The guards could never figure out how news traveled so fast through the campus. But nonetheless, it did, going from inmate to inmate. Gossip and news carried through the divisions as if on the wind, whispering their secrets to each inmate passed. Today the message was for James.

James heard a tapping on the cell bars next to him. He moved himself to the front of his stone box, holding his hand-held mirror through the bars. The guard was gone. His neighbor was tapping.

"What is it this time, mon?" James mumbled in his Jamaican accent.

"I got something for you. It was passed to Sal on the basketball court this morning. Says it's for you."

"All-righty then. What is it?"

The man passed James a crumpled, but still folded, note. He took the note and went back to sitting on his cot. Unfolding the paper, he noticed it was in code. A number given to every letter of the alphabet, the first number told the recipient where to start counting. For example, if the first number was 4, A was 4, B was 5, C was 6, and on through Z. The note would then consist of a series of numbers, which could be decoded off the first "marker number." If a note was ever confiscated or found while en route, the guard wouldn't know what it said.

James looked at the note, figured out the code, and started deciphering. When he got to the last number set, his dark black skin faded to two shades lighter. His knuckles went white as he crumpled the paper, balled it up, and tore it apart. Flinging the pieces of paper into his sink, James threw a match in after them.

He looked around his cinderblock walls and began to pray again. He chanted to himself silently, continuing to rock himself back and forth, back and forth. Why had he come to America? Why?

No man deserved this fate. He wasn't ready to die.

Chapter Two

Cook County Detention Center
October 2
1:58 P.M.

Dr. Mason Von Patton left the hospital early, hoping to arrive at the Cook County Jail by two o'clock. After fighting construction traffic, he arrived with a few minutes to spare.

Now, in the bowels of the oversized, overcrowded, and understaffed jail campus, the largest single-site jail in the country, the doctor moved silently through the underground concrete tunnels linking the eleven housing divisions. Six miles of drab institutional tunnels connected the housing divisions, making it easier for detainees and staff to move around the 97-acre campus, particularly during the brutal winters.

Dr. Von Patton emerged from the tunnel into Division II, a minimum-security dwelling resembling a long-neglected and budgetless vocational school building. He headed toward the tiny, secured examination room, where he hoped his first patient would be waiting.

The doctor opened the door to the cramped examination room and saw a young Hispanic man perched on the exam table. He grabbed his file from the plastic slot behind the door.

"Good afternoon . . . Miguel? Is it Miguel?" Dr. Von Patton repeated his pronunciation of the patient's name.

"Sì, yes," Miguel responded.

"I saw you last week, right?"

"Uh-huh, for blood work. You ordered lab work, remember?"

"That's right. Here it is now," the doctor announced, pulling the results from the file. He glanced briefly through the pages.

"Are you still having a hard time? Still tired and achy?"

"Yeah, it's getting worse I think."

"Your red blood cell count is low. I'm going to give you a subcutaneous injection of EPO, which just is a fancy term for a shot. Let me get George."

The doctor poked his head into the hallway and whistled for George, the physician's assistant who worked full time with the HIV/AIDS patients in his absence.

Dr. Von Patton volunteered at the jail coordinating the treatment of HIV-positive and AIDS patients. As an attending physician at City Memorial, he specialized in infectious diseases, specifically the research and treatment of AIDS patients.

A high-risk HIV population was usually defined as between one and two percent, and that number was blown away at Cook County Jail. The jail was the cream of the crop in terms of viral presence, offering percentages of infected inmates as high as five to six percent. This made the jail an ideal place for Dr. Von Patton to do some research while volunteering.

George, a large black man, finally appeared from around the corner where he had been smoking a cigarette.

"George, can you prepare an EPO shot for me?"

"No problem, doc," he replied cheerily. "I'll be right in with it."

"Great." The doctor turned back to his patient.

"What's going on with me?" Miguel asked anxiously.

"You're okay. It's just a low red blood cell count, I promise. We need to give you a couple of injections, and you'll be feeling better."

"How long do you think I got?" Miguel had been diagnosed with HIV more than five years ago.

"It's hard to say. The AZT is working wonders these days in HIV patients. People are living for many years."

Dr. Von Patton looked down at the countless track marks covering Miguel's arms. It was going to be hard to find a vein where he could inject the EPO. Miguel's veins were ravaged from years of heroin abuse. The doctor figured there probably wasn't much left to his immune system.

"But with this habit here, you've probably done about twenty years of damage to your body's defenses."

"What's wrong? Your eyes tell me something's wrong."

The doctor didn't respond.

"Is there something you're not telling me? Why are you looking so strange at me?"

"There's nothing I'm not telling you. Trust me. You just have to take care of yourself and make sure you take the AZT every day, that's it."

George tapped on the door to the tiny exam room, holding the EPO shot.

"You ready?"

"Sure am. Come on in."

Dr. Von Patton administered the shot quickly. Sadly, he had grown used to the needle-mark scarred arms of his patients.

"We'll do another blood test in a couple of weeks, see how things are looking. Okay?"

"Whatever you say, doc."

Miguel pulled his long underwear shirtsleeve down over his arm and tucked his tan county-issue scrub shirt into his pants.

"Later, doc," he called out as he exited the room.

Dr. Von Patton sighed.

"George, I don't know what we're going to do here. I

think they're going to need to hire a full-time guy soon. Other than yourself, that is. I've never seen anything like this. The growth here is overwhelming. The number of HIV-positive patients just keeps multiplying."

"It's all the needle-sharing out on the streets, coupled with the unprotected sex and gang rape going on in here. I'm surprised it's not worse." George shook his head in defeat. He moved away from the exam room door to try and rouse the next patient, who was napping in a chair in the makeshift waiting room. He turned back for a moment.

"Hey, how's the research paper going, by the way?"

Dr. Von Patton had been researching the spread of the HIV virus for months. He had his own lab at City Memorial, but his continued funding depended on him successfully wowing the National Institute of Health grantors.

"It's going well. Thanks for asking. It's important I finish it if I want to get more funding for the lab."

"That's a lot of pressure."

"Yes, it is. But I'll get there."

"What's it about, if you don't mind me asking?"

"It's confidential. Sorry, but you know how these things go. One leak and the whole thing could be ruined for me."

"Sure, cool. I understand."

"Who's up next?"

"It's supposed to be Bill Thompson, but we can't find him. He's not in Division X anymore."

Patients were transferred from divisions on a daily

basis to break up gang activity and, in the process, were regularly lost in the computerized tracking system, often for days at a time.

"So no one's gone for him?"

"Nope, can't find him. I've got Ashanti Jackson waiting, though."

"Fine, bring him in."

"Sure thing."

Chapter Three

Cook County Criminal Courthouse
26th Street and California Avenue
Chicago, Illinois
October 3
9:30 A.M.

The holding cells behind each courtroom were reminiscent of some sort of freak sideshow. Hallways connected all the courtrooms from the rear, hallways through which no one but court personnel, law enforcement officers, and defendants passed. The front of each holding tank was covered by a wall of metal bars, keeping the good from the evil, keeping the odd passerby from the criminals gathered behind the bars.

Metal benches lined the cinderblock walls of each holding cell, and a small metal toilet sitting open in the middle of the cell encouraged defendants to wait as long as they could before relieving themselves.

Everywhere a person looked there was only brown or dirty tan to see. Tan paint coated the cinderblock walls. The floor tiles were a darker shade of tan, and tan was the chosen color for the county uniforms the defendants wore. Even the courtrooms had been decorated in various shades of brown, either wood-lined or painted. The brown and tan served as a constant reminder that there was no oasis and no escape from the desolate desert island of the Cook County criminal justice buildings.

"Court will be back in session in one minute," the clerk's voice announced over the PA system.

A public defender lingered for a few extra minutes in the corridors behind the courtrooms, inhaling deeply from his Winston Light before grinding it out roughly beneath the heel of his ten-year-old Johnston & Murphy shoe. The attorney kicked the cigarette butt toward the cinderblock wall, its ashes leaving a trail across the floor, before it joined an assortment of earlier discarded butts.

The detainees in the holding cell behind Judge Doran's courtroom watched the attorney pass by as they nervously bounced their knees up and down. One inmate sat biting the skin around his fingernails. And then there was James.

James was staring straight ahead, breathing deeply, trying to stop his hands from shaking.

"Yo, Spiritman, what you so nervous for?" asked a young man the others called Boo.

"Nothin'. I'm not nervous about nothin'," James responded.

"You gonna try and cop a plea? You gonna take the deal?"

"Maybe."

"Whatchya in for anyway?" asked one of the other inmates.

"He's in for stealing a toilet, ain't that right, Spiritman? Tell 'em," Boo interjected.

"He's in for taking a toilet out of a building under rehab, right?" Boo's sidekick said.

The same group of inmates usually appeared on the same court dates, over and over again. The judge would usually set a case-status date ahead of time and give the entire group of inmates that same date for their next status call. So the inmates appeared together in bunches, often getting to know one another in the holding tanks behind the courtrooms.

In addition, the courtrooms had microphones that fed into the back hallways and the holding cell area, allowing the sheriff to know whom to bring out next and when court had returned to session. This meant most of the detainees knew the others' business.

The men were interrupted by the judge's voice over the microphone. "Court back in session. Let's have James Johannis."

The sheriff walked back to the holding cell. "All right, Johannis, let's go, your turn."

"Any last words of advice, sheriff?"

"Take the plea. Always go for the deal," the sheriff said, chuckling.

"See you later, Spritman!" Boo called out after him.

"Yah mon, I'll catch you later," James replied.

As he was led away to the courtroom, Boo remarked to one of his fellow inmates, "Man, that is one weird dude. Guy gets caught stealing a toilet. What a bum wrap. He's always chanting and shit, too. What's his deal anyway?"

"What are they offering him?"

"I heard the State wouldn't go under six, and he ain't taking it."

"The building was empty?"

"Yup, rehab project over on Fifty-fourth and Damen."

The voices behind James trailed off as he entered the courtroom on the third floor of the 26th and Cal courthouse, Judge Doran's courtroom, Courtroom 303.

The rooms, formerly administrative offices, had been gutted to make space for much-needed courtrooms. These lower-floor courtrooms were devoid of the upper-floor glamour. The upstairs courtrooms were like the ones in Hollywood, with wainscoted walls, twenty-foot ceilings, huge judicial benches and long wooden pews.

The lower-floor courtrooms were round with a thick pane of bullet proof glass separating the courtrooms from the spectator section. The people behind the panes overheard the court activity from the same speaker system connecting the waiting inmates to the court. Modern attorney tables seemed to grow right from the floor, one for the State and one for the defense.

James felt like he was in a giant fishbowl. As he walked across the courtroom, James glanced at the jury box on his right, where only one person sat today, a female sheriff. He approached Judge Doran's bench.

James stole a glimpse through the thick glass panes into the spectator section. He knew no one would be there for him, but it was hard to avoid the blank stares on the anxious faces behind the glass.

With James standing in front of his bench, Judge Doran shuffled through his papers, looking for James's file. The public defender stepped up, and the A.S.A. began to talk.

"Johannis. Charged with one count of burglary, a Class 2 felony, with a max of sixteen years. The State is recommending six. Previous convictions include one burglary and one misdemeanor theft. Defendant completed the boot camp program on the first burglary conviction. He's no longer eligible for boot camp."

"Okay, thank you. Miss Brown?" The judge nodded at the public defender to respond.

The public defender spoke loudly. "Your honor, the State's offer is unacceptable to my client. This man has only one prior felony conviction and his crime is, in essence, victimless. The building was empty, and this is a toilet we're talking about."

The judge addressed James directly. "Okay, I tell you

what I'm going to do. We'll do an *in camera* hearing—
that's a hearing in my chambers—where the State will
explain its rationale for a six-year minimum request,
defense explains its rationale, and then I will tell you
what I'll do, should you decide to plead guilty. Fair
enough?"

James nodded his assent.

This was Judge Doran's routine and all the defendants knew it. A Cook County judge didn't have to
take the State's recommendation. The judge could
hand out any sentence he felt appropriate, more or
less. Judge Doran always told the defendants what he
would do if the defendant took a plea bargain.

"All right, let's go back to chambers," Judge Doran
said.

Once in Judge Doran's chambers, James sat in the
chair closest to the window, open to the cool air. He
stared outside, temporarily drowning out the sound of
his public defender's voice. He knew this was his only
chance. It was now or never. He had to take it.

Go, go, go, he silently urged himself.

But he was frozen in his chair, his limbs stiff, they
would not respond.

Go damnit! Go now or die!

James, almost in a trance, jumped from his chair and
flung open the window. He tumbled through it in one
swift, if not graceful, motion. He was out, and falling
three flights down.

James hit the ground hard, rolling over several

times. He yelped and grabbed his ankle in pain. He had twisted it in the fall. With a burst of adrenaline, he picked himself up off the grass and ran.

He ran as fast as he could away from the building, his heart racing, his feet pounding one after the other against the pavement. He didn't look back.

But more importantly, he didn't look sideways as he rushed into the street.

James swung his head around when he heard the screech of the car's tires, just in time to catch the look of horror on the driver's face. Staring right at the driver, he realized what was about to happen.

Then everything went pitch black and James felt himself falling for the second time that morning. His head smacked against the pavement with a loud thud and his eyes shut instantly. He lay motionless in the middle of the street as a small crowd gathered.

Chapter Four

Essie folded the morning's newspaper and threw it in the trash on her way out the door. The news never had anything good to report, but today the latest tragedy was closer to home than she would have liked. The front page reported a second body had been discovered in an abandoned building down the street from her apartment. The sub-headline warned of similarities between the two recovered victims' bodies and suggested there might be more bodies still undiscovered. The article alluded to a possible serial killer, although the police department was denying that theory.

The women were described as having "high-risk" lifestyles. Both had been lured to their deaths, perhaps with the promise of drugs, their bodies found in nearby abandoned buildings.

"Police are not commenting on whether the murders are connected," Essie read aloud.

She didn't like that someone was out there assaulting women in her neighborhood, high-risk lifestyle or not. But, regardless of the dangers outside, it was time for her to go to work. She grabbed her can of Mace from a kitchen drawer, just to be cautious, and walked into the front hallway. From the closet, she chose her wool coat.

"Goodbye, you two!" she called to her daughter and the baby-sitter as she left the small apartment, still thinking about the news article.

How could this be happening in Pilsen? She lived in a decent community. Or so she had thought. Essie shook her head in disgust. Nowhere was safe anymore.

Nervous to be going out at night alone, she shuddered as she ran across the street to her parked car. She had to work the late shift. Looking back over her shoulder, she saw her ten-year-old daughter, Mariah, waving at her from the bedroom window. She hoped she would be okay with the sitter.

Essie rarely worked the late shift. Her seniority at the hospital allowed her to receive the more favorable hours most of the time. However, tonight she had agreed to switch with another nurse as a favor.

Why had she agreed to cover for Bonnie? She hated the night shift and hated having to leave Mariah home with a sitter all night, especially with some killer out lurking the streets.

Glancing at the digital clock on her dashboard, she realized she needed to hurry. Running late as usual, she pressed gently on the gas pedal, hoping to cut a couple of minutes off her short commute.

Essie, an infectious disease nurse, had worked in the ID Unit at the hospital for the past ten years. Working in the ID Unit had its benefits. Generally most of her patients were pleasant. The worst assignments were the Burn Unit or the Dialysis Unit. The patients couldn't help but resent the nurses, as their appearance always meant pain was to follow.

She pulled into a narrow space in the hospital lot, as close as she could get to the entrance. She shivered, her mind still on the killer haunting the city. Sighing, she grabbed her purse from the backseat, locked the car and walked briskly into the hospital and straight to the break room lockers.

"Hey Essie, I didn't know you were on duty tonight," said Sarah, one of the older nurses. Sarah was a large black woman of approximately fifty years and had extensive experience in dealing in a hospital setting. At the hospital she was a "floater," working wherever she was needed, for whatever unit happened to be momentarily understaffed—at least more than usual, as most of the underfunded hospital's units were regularly understaffed.

"I'm filling in for Bonnie, just for the night. Then I'm back to days."

"That's good, with your daughter and all. How is she, anyway?"

"Mariah is great, she's doing so well in school and everything."

"Good, glad to hear it. You still working the ID Unit?"

"Yes ma'am," Essie replied cheerfully.

"Well, have a good night. I'm in Trauma."

"Sorry to hear it." She smiled, knowing Sarah loved working Trauma, but equally loved groaning about her assignment there.

"Have a good one," Sarah called, exiting the break room.

Essie finished putting her purse and coat into her locker and headed for the ID Unit. Checking in with the head nurse, she reviewed her list of patients for the night.

Thirsty, she opened a can of soda, taking a long swallow. She fought her desire to call home to make sure everything was okay. She had been gone only half an hour and knew she needed to give the sitter some space.

"Time for work." She sighed to the empty room.

Taking another drink of soda, she pushed the door open harder than she expected and bumped right into Dr. Von Patton. Her drink spilled on his hands.

"Oh, excuse me, doctor. I'm so sorry, I didn't see you coming." Essie tried to wipe the doctor's hand.

"You know you're not supposed to have drinks on

28

the floor," Dr. Von Patton mumbled, exasperated and trying to wipe the sticky liquid from his hand.

"I was just about to throw it out, I swear."

"Just forget it, don't worry about it."

"What are you doing here so late anyway?" Essie asked.

Dr. Von Patton worked out of City Memorial Hospital but had privileges at Cook County Hospital, as did most of the doctors. She knew the doctor from the ID Unit, but usually he was only in during the daytime hours.

"I have a critical patient I needed to check on," the doctor replied hastily. "Excuse me, nurse," he said, brushing past Essie and inconsiderately knocking her aside.

Essie was surprised. Dr. Von Patton was usually very polite and courteous. She liked him quite a bit, more than most of the other doctors, who often spoke down to the nurses. Dr. Von Patton was cordial and never condescended to her.

Tonight however, the doctor was clearly in a rush. One of the busier doctors, he managed to run his own research lab, did patient consultations at the FORBES Center, and still completed his hospital rounds.

He had seemed overly agitated by the small spill, but she decided to forget about it and went over to the nurses' station to check her patient list again and prepare for what promised to be a long night.

Chapter Five

1918 South Indiana
Chicago, Illinois
October 8
5:35 P.M.

After attending mass early that morning, Dr. Von Patton spent the rest of the afternoon and the better part of the early evening preparing for his party. The doctor's parties were infamous, drawing most of the neighborhood. He furnished his guests with nothing but the best, often supplying top-shelf liquors and gourmet foods. All the neighbors knew him for his fabulous entertaining as well as the great gossip his parties provided.

Among the doctor's assortment of posh fellow community members was none other than the city's mayor, who had even been a guest himself on prior occasion.

Perhaps he might visit this evening, Dr. Von Patton thought excitedly. He planned to start the festivities around six o'clock. He threw all kinds of parties, using a variety of themes, everything from barbecues to all-out galas. Tonight he had planned for the latter. He sent out engraved invitations for the dressy affair to almost everyone he knew and invited his guests to bring others. It promised to be a grand event.

He had reserved some of the finest violinists the city offered and the caterer would be serving rack of lamb and Chilean sea bass. A variety of pâtés and sweetbreads would be available as well. He had selected the menu himself after careful thought.

He looked in his hallway mirror, straightening his silver locks with the palm of his hand, eagerly anticipating the arrival of his guests. He didn't have long to wait.

The doorbell rang and the first group of party-goers poured into the house, raving about his beautiful décor and exclaiming at his exquisite taste.

Dr. Von Patton fancied himself as a character out of an F. Scott Fitzgerald novel. He believed himself charming, entertaining, yet mysterious all at the same time. Unattached, the doctor used the parties to satiate his desire for company.

Truth be told, the doctor didn't much care for intimacy. His work kept him so busy that female companionship was not an option, not that he didn't enjoy the women who often showed up at his parties. He always appreciated the company of a beautiful woman, just not long enough for a real relationship to develop.

People were starting to arrive in droves and the house quickly filled with the sounds of laughter, chatter, and music. As the doctor roamed the hallways, chatting casually with his many guests, he noticed a young woman, a first-time visitor. She was staring curiously at a frame on the wall.

"Good evening," he said, interrupting her gaze.

"Oh, hello," the young woman sputtered, turning to find herself staring directly into the steel eyes of her handsome host.

"I'm Dr. Mason Von Patton. I live here."

"How charming to meet you. I'm Delphine Groves, Charlotte Groves's daughter. I was wondering if I might have the good fortune to make your acquaintance. My mother has told me so many good things about you. I must say, so far, they all seem to be true. Your home is positively beautiful. Everything so carefully selected."

"Thank you very much. I appreciate your kindness, deserved or not." The doctor smiled graciously. "And I must say what a delightful name you have, Delphine, not very common at all."

"Oh, thank you. I never much cared for it, to be quite honest."

"Wasn't there a famous Delphine from New Orleans once?"

"Yes, actually. Infamous. The story is horrid, though. Really, I'd rather not repeat it."

"Well then, I shouldn't ask you to. Although nothing about such a charming and vibrant young woman could be horrid." The doctor flirted with his young guest.

Blushing, Delphine turned her head away, slightly embarrassed.

"May I ask what it is that intrigued you on the wall?"

"I was admiring your framed stamps, particularly those that have been postmarked."

"Ah, yes. They are German, from 1923."

"Do you mind if I ask, aren't they of more value when they're unused?"

"That's usually the case, yes. However, this particular series and year, the stamps are more valuable if postmarked. You see, during the war no one used postage. No one was mailing anything, couldn't afford it. So to find a postmarked stamp from this year . . . well, it's very rare."

"I see. I had no idea. I have to admit I know nothing of stamps."

"I suppose it's not common knowledge. I myself was mostly intrigued by the notion that something used and discarded, of no value at all to anyone, could end up being more valuable than that which is new. Interesting, I think."

"Yes, it is," Delphine agreed. "Do you collect stamps regularly?"

"I do. I find it an incredibly peaceful and relaxing way to spend the little free time I have."

"I can see how it would be."

"May I offer you something else to drink?" the doctor asked, noticing she had finished her wine.

"I would love another glass of chardonnay. Thank you so much."

"My pleasure."

Dr. Von Patton wandered away to find the wine steward and fetch the young woman another glass.

Early the next morning Dr. Von Patton awoke with a start. He must have dozed off in his den after his guests had left. He blinked his eyes open, trying to adjust them, then looked at his wristwatch. It was seven in the morning.

"Monday already," he moaned aloud.

Perhaps he would go out for breakfast. He had been having difficulty sleeping lately and was surprised he had fallen asleep in the stiff leather armchair.

The doctor went into the bathroom to wash his face before taking himself out for blintzes. He dressed quickly and grabbed his research notes on the way out the door, planning to read them over breakfast.

As he approached his early model Mercedes, he felt a hand on his arm, a gentle tug.

"Excuse me, sir?"

He turned over his shoulder to see who was disturbing him this early in the morning.

"Dr. Mason Von Patton?"

"Yes?"

"Chicago Police. You're under arrest, sir," the young officer announced.

"What? For what?"

"I have a warrant for your arrest . . ." The officer's voice trailed off, and Dr. Von Patton didn't hear anything past "arrest." The officer turned the doctor around and leaned him against the car. He patted him down, performing a routine weapons check.

"Sir, you have the right to remain silent. Anything you say can and will be used against you in a court of law. You have the right to an attorney. If you can't afford an attorney, one will be appointed for you." The officer cuffed the doctor and led him to his squad car. He pressed the doctor's head down gently but firmly, guiding him into the backseat.

Dr. Von Patton was aghast. He was being arrested and apparently was on his way to the police station.

"What are you arresting me for?" he was still asking as the officer eased the car out into the empty street.

Chapter Six

Cook County Hospital
Chicago, Illinois
October 9
9:27 A.M.

Sarah found out she had been assigned to the jail section of Cook County Hospital for the next several weeks. One of the regular nurses was out on maternity leave and Sarah was filling in. She had worked in the jail section on previous occasions, so she already knew the additional rules and regulations required for this special set of patients.

The jail section of Cook County Hospital was the temporary home for inmates awaiting or recovering from surgery, or for those who were too ill to be cared for in the jail's medical facilities. Which, in Sarah's opinion, meant any inmate with more than a common cold. Nonetheless, not many inmates found themselves at Cook County Hospital, not unless something serious had happened. And for those folks, they were put in the jail section, a secured area of the hospital specifically reserved for the care of the incarcerated.

The head nurse was going through the patient roster with Sarah. "James Johannis. This guy has officially found himself a new temporary home in our section. Suffered from multiple abrasions and injuries, patient underwent emergency surgery and was yanked from death's grip."

Sarah flipped through his chart. "Escape attempt?"

"Yeah, guy jumped out of an open window three floors up."

She continued reading. Minor concussion. He had just been transferred from ICU that day.

She walked over to James's bed. Still incoherent, he was hooked up to a heart monitor. His eyes were half-closed and seemed to be fluttering slightly. He looked eerie, lying under the florescent lights, staring up at her.

"Hey there, Mr. Johannis," Sarah said to the half corpse lying beneath the crisp white sheets.

"I'm Sarah. Sarah Thomas. And I'm going to be your nurse. And it looks like it might be for a while. So we might as well get to know one another. Okay?"

Sarah hummed gently under her breath as she checked the catheter needle in James's hand. The sodium drip was full and his vital signs were stable. At least for now. She hoped he would make it. He was too young to die.

James hadn't shown any signs of coherency in days. After being dragged into the emergency room, he had slipped into a coma. They had stabilized him and turned him over to Sarah.

"And Sarah will get you well," she murmured in the sleeping man's ear. "Yes sir, Mr. Johannis. You're not going to leave us that easily. Not on old Sarah's watch."

Making sure James's body rested in a comfortable position, she moved on to another patient. She'd have to keep a close eye on him, though. No telling when he might come around.

Chapter Seven

District 1, Central Station
11 E. State Street
Chicago, Illinois
October 9
10:12 A.M.

Dr. Von Patton had been arrested and brought to Central Station on 11th and State. There he had been subjected to the humiliating process of being photographed and fingerprinted. And he had been fully informed of the charges against him: two counts of criminal sexual assault.

One of the police officers had taken his personal belongings from him in exchange for a property inventory slip. Handing him the slip, the young officer glanced at the bottle of pills they had retrieved from the doctor's pocket.

"It's Tegretol, a phenobarbital. For epileptic seizures," Dr. Von Patton offered.

"Did I ask?" the officer replied, uninterested. He had already noted the doctor's possessions on the property invoice, including the medication.

"Yes, your facial expression did," the doctor responded.

"Walk in front of me," another officer instructed Dr. Von Patton. "We're going down the hall to your right."

Dr. Von Patton did as he was told, allowing himself to be placed in an interrogation room. He looked around the dirty institutional room, in disbelief that he was in this situation. The room smelled of stale sweat, urine, and body odor. He couldn't stand it.

He wasn't alone for long. A man around his own age came into the room and introduced himself.

"I'm Detective Marshall," he said, seating himself across from the doctor. "I'm going to explain to you why you're here."

"That would be nice."

"You've been charged with criminal sexual assault."

"That much I've been told."

"Two of your patients have complained about some of your actions. They claim they were subjected to unnecessary tests as well as unprofessional and nonroutine questioning about their sexual lives."

"What? That's ridiculous. Who? Which patients?"

"Two female patients. Both twenty-something. Said

you touched them inappropriately during their exams, that sort of thing." The detective was taking a calm and rational approach with the doctor.

Marshall tried to empathize with him. "It's understandable. Hell, if I were a doctor and had good-looking women coming into my office taking their clothes off all the time . . . I don't blame you." Detective Marshall chuckled before continuing with his questions. "These patients, one says you pushed her down on an exam table. You know anything about that?"

"No, I don't know anything about that."

The detective changed his tone. "This can be easy for you or it can be difficult. It's your choice. This is your chance to tell me your side of the story. These women have made some serious allegations against you. Two women. With similar stories."

Dr. Von Patton started to shake. His eyes glazed over and he went completely blank for a moment. Then, just as quickly, he snapped back into the present.

"Are you okay?" the detective asked.

"No, I'm not. I have a prescription for Tegretol, for seizures, and your fellow officers took it from me when I was brought in."

"Why don't you just tell me what happened and I'll get you your stuff back right away," Detective Marshall said.

"Why don't I not? Why don't I make a request to talk with my attorney. Meaning you can stop questioning me. Now."

"Look, Dr. Von Patton. This is a serious charge. A Class 1 felony. I'm giving you an opportunity to talk to me now."

"I want to speak with my attorney. I will not answer any questions, nor will I speak with anyone until I have talked with my lawyer."

"Fine, if that's the way you want it." The detective rose from his chair, pushing himself away from the table.

"Yes, thank you. That is very much what I would prefer."

"Someone will be right in for you. We'll get you your attorney." The detective left, knowing he was unable to press the doctor for further information once he made a request for legal assistance.

Dr. Von Patton watched the detective leave the room. He squirmed uncomfortably in his chair, still wondering what the hell was going on. Having been up half the night, he felt drained. The few hours he had slept in the den chair weren't of much consolation to him now. He needed a pill, too. It wasn't good for him to go without sleep, food, or his medication. His attorney had better get him out of here soon.

"The police didn't want to risk anything with you. You're older, obviously educated. They weren't going to continue a line of questioning once you asked for me. But it's a good thing you asked right away."

"Thanks, Tom. I appreciate your coming down here."

"It's no problem, really. I have to be in court in a couple of hours, though. So I'll have to talk with you about this later today."

Dr. Von Patton had been brought before a judge first thing after his arrest for a bail bond hearing. His attorney and friend, Tom Foster, had come down for the hearing and Dr. Von Patton had been released on bail. The two were now leaving the courtroom.

"I can't handle your case. You know that, right? This isn't my area of practice. I know nothing about criminal law. Barely studied it in law school. I'm strictly real estate and tax."

"I know, Tom. You've done enough. Could you recommend someone?"

"That I can definitely do for you. I know a couple of good criminal defense attorneys. I'll call you later this afternoon, see how you're doing and give you a couple of names and numbers."

"Again, thank you for help. I can't tell you how grateful I am. I have no idea why this is happening," he added.

Dr. Von Patton was tired, hungry, and in a state of shock. His disarray wasn't lost on Tom.

"I'm sure you'll get this all straightened out. You'll get it worked out. Whatever it is that's going on here." Tom put his hand over the doctor's shoulder. "It's too bad, especially for this to happen to someone like you. With all you do. It's terrible."

Tom looked at his watch. "I'm sorry, I've got to run. I've got to be in a zoning hearing shortly. I'd love to give you a ride, but I'm headed the other way. Do you have money for a cab?"

Dr. Von Patton nodded.

"Okay, I'll call you later," Tom promised.

He rushed down the stairs of the building, leaving Dr. Von Patton staring after him, wondering how he was going to get home.

Book II

The Counselor

Chapter Eight

19 South LaSalle Street
Chicago, Illinois
October 26
10:46 A.M.

Janna finished unpacking the last of her boxes. She had moved into the small office over a month ago, but had just started settling in. She looked around the little room. Not bad, she thought.

Her office was located in the Loop in one of Chicago's historical buildings. The building could be entered only by walking through an old steel gate and going down a cobblestone alley. Janna liked the traditional feel of it, like she was part of history herself.

Somewhere on her desk, her phone was ringing. Rifling through her files and papers, she finally discovered the cordless handset and answered on the fourth ring, just beating the voice mail system.

"Janna Scott," she answered.

"Hello?"

"Yes, hello. Can I help you?"

"Is this Janna Scott?"

"This is she. What can I do for you?"

"My name is Dr. Mason Von Patton. I was referred to you by Tom Foster."

"Good old Tom. How is he these days, anyway?"

"He's fine. Look, Ms. Scott, if it's all the same to you, I don't much care for small talk. I find it wastes a tremendous amount of time when taken as a whole. So, if you don't mind I'll get right to the point."

"Fine by me," she answered, thinking the guy sounded awfully pompous. "Tell me your problem and I'll see if I can help you."

"I've been arrested and charged with criminal sexual assault, whatever that means. I'm looking to obtain legal representation."

"I see. Are you currently out on bond?"

"Yes."

Janna's mind went into overdrive. A doctor charged with criminal sexual assault. It could be interesting. Although sex crimes had never been her favorite as an Assistant State's Attorney. They weren't anyone's.

At the State's Attorney's office, the sex cases were divided up among the A.S.A.s and each attorney stayed with his or her case. Unlike the routine felony, which stayed with a courtroom, no matter which attorney was swapped in.

Due to the sensitive nature of the matter and the difficulty of proving the facts, the sex cases were better off not jumping from attorney to attorney. If switched around, each new attorney on the case had to keep relearning the facts and regaining the victim's trust.

Sex cases were also extremely complicated to try. There were usually no witnesses and and the victims were reluctant. But that was from the State's viewpoint, and Janna was no longer a prosecutor.

She had opened her own practice, and for the time being, her practice consisted of mainly criminal defense work. Janna still wasn't sure she had made the right decision, but with seven years of prosecuting under her belt and some seventy jury trials later, she wasn't cut out for much else.

"Doctor Von . . . I'm sorry, what did you say your last name was again?"

"Von Patton. Mason Von Patton."

"Dr. Von Patton, why don't you tell me a couple of things about what happened and if I can help you out with representation, we'll set up an appointment."

"All right, what can I tell you?"

"First, when were you arrested?"

"About two weeks ago, on Monday morning."

"And was there a warrant?"

"Yes, I was arrested at my home as I was trying to get into my car."

"Where's that?"

"My home?"

"Yes."

"It's on South Indiana, around the 1900 block."

Janna paused, changing the subject momentarily. "Doesn't the mayor live in that area?"

"Yes, down the block."

"That's what I thought." Remembering the doctor's earlier admonition, she continued. "Anyway, what police station were you brought to, if you recall?"

"Eleventh and State."

"Okay. And you had your initial appearance before the judge that morning and posted bond, correct?"

"That is correct."

"What were the exact charges?"

"Two counts of criminal sexual assault."

"When did the alleged assaults occur?"

"According to the charges, just this past summer, in July."

"And who are the alleged victims?"

"A patient. Two patients, actually."

"Your patients?"

"Yes, both are my patients."

"What kind of medicine do you practice?"

"I am an infectious disease doctor."

"Uh-huh. Well, I think I can help you out. Why don't you come in to see me and bring all your paperwork. I'll also need a retainer."

"How much?"

"Five thousand dollars, as a retainer. You can bring

in the difference between that and your bond if you want. I have forms here where you can sign the bond you posted over to me, if that's easier for you."

"That won't be necessary. I'll bring you a check. When are you available?"

Janna glanced at the office calendar on her desk. The real question was when was she not available. Business hadn't really kicked into high gear yet, and although she wasn't looking forward to defending a sex offender, she needed the cash.

"You can come in tomorrow afternoon if you like, or first thing Monday morning."

"I'll be in Monday morning. What time?"

"Does ten o'clock work for you?"

"Perfect. I'll see you then."

Janna gave her new client directions and hung up the phone, still doubting her choice to enter private practice. But it was too late to change her mind now.

Although she enjoyed prosecuting, the politics of the State's Attorney's Office had been too much to handle in the end. She had been forced to make a move.

There were few opportunities for women in the office, and even fewer for women with no political connections. It was either become a judge or enter private practice, and since the political track wasn't working in her favor, Janna had chosen private practice. Her own.

She had opened her doors more than a month ago, and her office showed its youth in her decorative choices. She had hung her diplomas in a corner, where they wouldn't seem ostentatious to potential clients.

She had also chosen a vintage poster reprint for above the credenza behind her desk. The poster depicted a stack of books with the scales of justice in the background, definitely appropriate. The office was sparse, but so was business.

As for her staff, she shared a secretary with the other office space renters; and for the investigatory end of things, she was on her own.

Chapter Nine

Cook County Hospital Parking Lot
Chicago, Illinois
October 27
7:41 P.M.

The cool wind blew through Essie's hair as she ran out to her car. Dust particles flew into her eyes, causing her to squint. She hugged herself, trying to retain whatever body heat she could. She had parked farther away than usual that morning, all the way at the end of the parking lot.

The October night air served as a chilling reminder that another Chicago winter was just around the corner. There were barely any leaves left on the trees, and the atmosphere was perfect for the fast approaching Halloween. Mariah wanted to go as an angel this year.

Essie jumped, startled, as she felt a hand grab her arm.

"Excuse me, ma'am." The offensive man pled, "Do you have any spare change for me? I'm just trying to get me something to eat."

The man's eyes were bloodshot, his one hand clutching a tattered copy of *Streetwise*, the newsletter run by the homeless. He was noticeably missing the required vendor's badge. The man smelled awful, his odor overpowering even through the brisk fall wind.

"I'm sorry. I don't have anything for you tonight. I can't help," Essie said, trying to shrug him off.

"Please ma'am. I really could use a hot meal," the man begged again, still hanging on to her coat sleeve. He was starting to scare her, moving in closer.

"Let me go. Let go of my arm," she said loudly, trying to shake him off her wool overcoat.

The smell of stale urine and alcohol emanated from his pores and clothing, overpowering her. She tried to move away, keeping her eyes on the vagrant man as she hurried off toward her car.

"God bless you, ma'am! The Lord be with you tonight, you hear!" He was yelling after her, and she could feel his eyes following her to the car.

It was so frustrating, these homeless people wandering the streets, some of them half crazy or more. She wanted to help, but she had no money to spare. She was barely going to be able to get dinner for her and Mariah. Life as a single mother wasn't easy. She knew she had no room to feel sorry for herself, though. It could be far worse.

Nonetheless, the man scared her, almost forcing her to stop. His eyes had been so red, and his tone so imposing. It was frightening. She wanted to give him money just to get him to move away from her.

Essie climbed into her Escort, vowing never to park so far from the hospital entrance again. She turned the key and the engine roared up on the first try, thankfully. That was one thing she didn't need tonight, a broken-down car. Eager to get home to Mariah and still needing to stop at the store, she peeled off down the street.

After driving only a few blocks, she was accosted for a second time, this time by the red and blue flashing lights of the squad cars blocking her way. The cars lined the west side of Ashland Street. A patrolman was redirecting her out of her lane and around the parked squad cars. Traffic was temporarily stopped as he let the northbound traffic pass.

Essie peered through the passenger window of her car, curious as to what all the commotion was about. The medical examiner's van was parked on the street among the squad cars. They were all in front of a broken-down building, the windows boarded up.

Not another one, she thought. Essie crossed her heart, silently saying a prayer for the victim that had undoubtedly been found in the building. The officer directing traffic was staring right at her.

"Move it out, lady!" he yelled.

She snapped her head up. She must have blanked out for a minute. She rolled down her window.

"It's not another woman, is it?" she asked.

"Can't say anything, ma'am. Please keep moving."

She pressed on the gas pedal and drove away from the crime scene. She gave the officer a backward glance in her rearview mirror. Her gaze locked on the flashing lights behind her, mesmerized by their eerie glow. This was terrible, if the police had in fact found another body, and again in her neighborhood.

She gasped, clucking her tongue against her front teeth. She looked up in time to slam on the brakes. She had almost run a red light. The car behind her honked angrily as she jerked to an abrupt halt.

She looked around the empty street in front of her. She had promised to help Mariah with her costume that night. She needed to focus.

This was not the time for a mental sabbatical, which Essie had been taking more and more of lately. Ever since Joe died she flustered more easily. She pulled herself together and drove away from the disturbing scene, eager for the safety of her little apartment.

Chapter Ten

Hastings and Ashland Avenue
Chicago, Illinois
October 27
10:24 P.M.

Detective Jack Stone rubbed his temples and scanned the girl's broken naked body, sprawled in the rubble, meaninglessly discarded. She looked almost inhuman. Her legs were twisted beneath her, and her skin looked translucent under the officer's flashlights. In the little light available Detective Stone could see red burn marks around her ankles, which indicated her feet must have been bound at some point.

A noose was still fastened around her neck, tied in some sort of boatman's knot or something. He couldn't tell. There was a lot of bruising around her neck. From that, he guessed the rope had been the final messenger of death.

He briefly examined her appearance, her hair, jewelry, and nails. It seemed this woman, like the others, had worked in the sex industry. She was either a prostitute or possibly a stripper, judging from her muscular legs.

Her body had been found in the basement of an abandoned building, of which the area had plenty to offer. The police had received an anonymous phone call, alerting them to the dead woman's body, which was lying rotting in the broken down building. The concrete floor was drenched in water and trash. The basement had apparently been flooded by the recent rain. It certainly wasn't going to help the evidence the crime lab technicians were busy salvaging.

What a mess, Detective Stone thought. He glanced around the concrete hole. They'd be lucky to pull anything of use out of this place, other than the body.

The building was a crack house. It was probably one of the junkies who called the cops, upset his turf had been intruded upon. Once the body had been removed, the junkies would come right back.

Stone looked around at the litter and debris scattered across the cement floor. A rat scampered over one of the ceiling pipes just above his head, startling him. He shone his flashlight at the ceiling. Nothing but wooden floorboards and pipes.

He shone his flashlight back around the basement.

The place was busier than Mike's cop bar on a Saturday night. It was a lot of people for a dead hooker.

"I didn't know we even had this many guys on the force," he joked aloud, to no one in particular. Stone looked around for his partner, Arnie, but didn't see him. He must be outside talking to the responding officers, Stone thought.

The responding officers had roped off the house and secured the area hours earlier, but the crime scene was still being processed. In the basement, the photographer's flash bulbs were leaving blind spots in Stone's eyes. Stone noticed the medical examiner lingering around, waiting for the evidence technician to finish. He watched the technicians pick through the basement collecting evidence, and he yawned. He moved around the outer perimeter of the scene, peering down at the woman.

He thought he saw something in the woman's hand, and stepped over to see what it was, bending his slightly graying head over her half-open hand.

"Hey fellas, I think we've got something over here in the girl's hand," he yelled.

The Chicago Police Department's evidence technician came over and opened the woman's palm, removing a piece of metal. As he held it up, even in the dim light Jack could see it was a cross. The woman had been holding a cross in the palm of her hand. It was still attached to a rope necklace that had been wound through her fingers.

"Got it," the technician said as he removed the cross from her hand and put it in a paper bag.

He folded the top of the paper bag and left. The medical examiner assigned to pick up the body walked over. Stone had been a homicide detective for more than ten years and recognized him from previous cases.

"Hey, Carl, how are you?"

"I'd be better if I was home in bed right now."

"Isn't that the truth."

Carl started to prepare the body for transport to the morgue.

"So what do you think?"

"Marbling has already started. She's probably been dead for a while."

"I figured from the smell," Jack mumbled.

"She has bruising and lacerations all over her face and neck. The bruising is probably from the rope." The medical examiner sighed, briefly examining the woman's beaten face.

"There's a cross carved into her stomach here. She also has some strange markings on her breasts. I can't see much in this light, though. It looks like there might be some markings on her inner thighs," Carl said. He and his partner lifted the woman into the black body bag.

"Looks worse than the last two found over here."

"We'll know soon enough."

"Yes, we will." Detective Stone coughed into his hand as he turned away from the body. He walked up the cellar stairs into the cool Chicago air and took a deep breath. He never got used to it—the butchered bodies of the city's dead. It still disturbed him, especially young women.

He walked back to his car, stopping to talk to one of the R.O.s along the way.

"What do you think, detective?"

"I think we've got another one."

"Same guy?" the younger officer asked.

"Looks like it. And he's getting worse, more violent. By the way, nice work on securing our crime scene," Stone said to the young officer. He nodded his approval before getting into his unmarked Chevy Caprice. Not much else he could do here tonight.

He found Arnie and told him he was headed home.

"I've been up since the middle of last night. I'll fill out paperwork tomorrow morning. The autopsy report won't be back for at least a few days, depending on the situation at the morgue. Not much else I can do here tonight."

"You get your beauty rest. Take the car. I'll see you tomorrow," Arnie said.

This was the third body in two weeks.

Stone shook his head. He knew he needed to rest, his eyes were heavy and the coffee he had been swallowing down all night wasn't keeping him awake anymore.

He needed to sleep.

Chapter Eleven

1918 South Indiana
Chicago, Illinois
October 30
8:56 A.M.

Dr. Mason Von Patton examined his face closely in the antique mirror, plucking an errant nose hair with a pair of tweezers. His steel gray eyes stared back at him, offended by the sharp glare of the bathroom bulbs. He had been meaning to put a dimmer in the bathroom, but hadn't gotten to it yet.

He hummed Mendelssohn to himself, transfixing his gaze on his individual pores, looking at each one under the bright light. Dr. Von Patton was waiting for his water to boil, so he could pour himself a cup of morning tea.

The doctor was meticulous about his appearance, his personal hygiene, and about cleanliness overall. His patterns fell just short of obsessive. He washed his hands, scrubbing them under the tap water, and flossed his teeth twice for good measure. Glancing at his reflection once more in the mirror, he turned from the bathroom and went to dress himself. He knew he had a stressful day ahead of him.

With his tea, he returned to his bedroom and stood before the open closet. He flipped through the clothes, unable to decide what to wear for his meeting with his new counsel.

He wanted to appear intelligent, but he also wanted to seem humble, at least for the first meeting. He wanted to ingratiate himself to this woman, his savior, or so he hoped.

He chose a French blue shirt and a pair of olive wool Armani pants. He felt he had selected a suitable ensemble. Average, yet tasteful. More importantly, his chosen attire was nonthreatening. He looked harmless, and his demeanor would suggest the same. And if there was one thing he definitely wanted, it was to leave his attorney with the impression he was a harmless man.

After removing the slacks from their hanger, he decided to fluff the shirt momentarily in the dryer to remove some of the heavy starching. It looked too harsh, too crisp.

Finished with his tea and still thirsty, Dr. Von Patton poured himself a glass of fresh orange juice and walked over to the dryer. As he took a large gulp from the glass, he could feel his jaw muscles working, strong and masculine. There was no question about it, the doctor was a very attractive man, with distinguished features. And he knew it.

He put his shirt in the dryer and stared at the light flickering through the glass in the metal door as the drum spun around, losing himself in his thoughts for a moment. As the light flickered before his eyes, he felt a sharp pain shoot through his head.

That was when it hit.

Dr. Von Patton's glass of orange juice fell and shattered on the floor, and his hands clenched into fists. His body began to convulse uncontrollably. His mind went blank and images began to flash in front of his eyes. He fell to his knees before the dryer, his heart pulsating and his head throbbing. His eyeballs rolled back into his head.

His body convulsed for what seemed like minutes on end, but in reality the convulsions lasted for only thirty seconds or less. Then it was over, as quickly as it had begun.

His forehead was pounding. He grabbed his head and swayed back and forth on the floor in front of the dryer, trying to soothe his disrupted body and mind.

He hated the seizures.

Ever since falling from a set of playground monkey bars as a child he experienced them. As a result of the fall, he had received a frontal lobe injury and the doctors told him he would have episodic seizures for the rest of his life.

Luckily, they never rose to the level of grand mal seizures. They were more like fits, brief blackouts. Although lately they seemed to be occurring more frequently, and they also seemed to be worsening.

Dr. Von Patton could never recall the seizures, or what happened during them, just the way he felt afterward. And right now he felt horrible. He looked at the dryer, remembering he had been staring at the flickering light behind the door when the fit started. Closing his eyes, he could still see the flashing light.

He opened his eyes and noticed a large dent in the dryer door. That was odd. He must have struck the door during the fit, or when he fell to the floor. Dr. Von Patton had not suffered from convulsions until recently, so this was all new to him. He was used to the brief memory lapses, but convulsions?

The doctor removed his shirt from the dryer and returned to his bedroom to finish dressing. He popped a Tegretol and looked at the clock.

Dr. Von Patton had to meet Janna in one hour. He had better get moving.

Chapter Twelve

19 South LaSalle Street
Chicago, Illinois
October 30
10:02 A.M.

Janna ran some background checks on Dr. Von Patton before he arrived at her office. Using Westlaw, her on-line legal research program, she verified his address, determined his medical license was current, and even checked his property assets.

She also checked the court records to verify the charges as well as the preliminary hearing date. The preliminary hearing would be Janna's first chance to get the doctor's case dismissed. But it was a slim chance.

And that was only if she decided to represent him.

She still needed to hear his side of the story before agreeing to take his case. Nonetheless, it was always best to do some preparation before a prospective client came in for a first meeting.

Janna's first step was to find out what happened on the days the doctor allegedly assaulted his patients. In order to cross-examine the victims, she needed to do some story checking with her client.

Janna turned away from her computer screen. Someone was tapping on her door, gently pushing it open. A little surprised by the intrusion, she wondered why the receptionist hadn't phoned back. She must be away from her desk again, Janna thought, annoyed.

"Hello?" she called out to the man who was entering her small office.

"Yes, hello. I'm Dr. Mason Von Patton. We spoke on the phone the other morning."

"Yes, please come in and have a seat." Janna motioned him toward her guest chairs.

Janna watched the doctor as he sat in front of her second-hand desk. Though slightly older, he was handsome. He exuded confidence, but contrary to what she had thought on the phone, he did not come off as arrogant in person. The doctor was neatly dressed and his appearance was conservative yet stylish. He looked tired and definitely distraught. He crossed his legs, straightened his pant leg and made himself comfortable in the chair.

"Did you bring copies of your arrest report, or whatever they gave you?"

"Yes, I did." The doctor handed her a manila file folder.

"Everything I was given is contained in that file. I made copies for myself. You can keep what's there."

"Great." Janna took the file from him and briefly glanced through its contents. There was the arrest report, an invoice for property taken at the time of arrest, and a bail bond receipt.

"Why don't you tell me briefly what's going on here, why you were arrested?" she asked.

"That's just it. I really have no idea. I don't have an inkling as to what these women are talking about."

Janna sighed audibly. Another innocent defendant. Weren't they all? America had amassed jails full of innocents, it seemed.

"Okay then. Why don't we start with the women? Who are they? Do you know them?"

"Yes. They're both patients of mine. They were patients for no more than a year. Relatively new patients."

"What kind of medicine do you practice?"

"Infectious disease."

"How old are the patients, if you know?"

"Both in their twenties."

"And what are they saying?"

"We haven't spoken with one another," the doctor replied, "but from what I gathered at the police station, they're saying that I molested them in some manner. Inappropriate touching and questioning, that sort of thing."

"I see. What sort of touching?" Janna asked gently.

68

"I don't know. I truly do not know what these women are claiming."

"Criminal sexual assault, what you're charged with, requires penetration of some sort. Simple inappropriate touching, or fondling, isn't enough to sustain a charge of criminal sexual assault where the victim is over seventeen. They must be claiming you penetrated them in some manner," Janna said.

"This whole thing is crazy."

Janna glanced again at his papers.

"I think the police mentioned something about unnecessary anal examinations," the doctor finally said.

"Unnecessary anal examination?" She raised her eyebrows.

"It's all ludicrous. I would never recommend something that wasn't absolutely necessary or prudent."

"What would be the general procedure for this type of patient?"

"A number of things might be done. Blood work, a urine sample might be taken. I would conduct a physical examination. A lot of possibilities, depending on the symptoms."

"Who approved the charges on this?" Janna wondered aloud.

An Assistant State's Attorney from the Felony Review Unit had to approve the charges on any felony case before charges were formally brought. The State's Attorney's Office didn't want to be prosecuting cases for which it didn't have sufficient evidence.

"Probably one of the infamous A.S.A.s who took

the bar four times before passing, but has a well-connected father," Janna mumbled, more to herself than the doctor.

"Any priors?" she asked him.

"Priors?"

"Prior arrests."

"No, none," he replied flatly.

"You're being charged with improper examinations, basically," Janna decided, having briefly assessed the facts, but knowing she needed to do some research. At this point, she knew the legwork would be up to her.

The poor man before her looked utterly confused and dismayed. She knew she would take his case, even though she didn't care for the facts or his minimal knowledge about the circumstances leading to his arrest. That coupled with an absolute lack of desire to cooperate with her, yes . . . he would make for a typical criminal defendant.

But she had little choice; her practice wasn't exactly booming. She needed the money and he was a well-paid doctor.

"Let me explain briefly to you what will happen next. The court has set a date for a preliminary hearing in less than two weeks. They will be looking to establish probable cause, or whether there is good reason for these charges to have been brought, basically whether this case should be in the court system at all. As a rule of thumb, the court almost always finds probable cause. A dismissal at the preliminary hearing stage in a sex case is rare. If probable cause is found, we'll have to start preparing for trial. I will request all the information the State has through discovery.

"I also have to ask you about plea bargain possibilities. The State might be willing to lower the charges due to the circumstances. It doesn't look like they have a real strong case. Maybe aggravated battery, maybe even two straight battery charges."

The doctor lifted his head from his hands.

"Absolutely not. Not a chance. I will not plead guilty to anything. Is that understood? I heard you know the system up and down and most of the A.S.A.s who work in it. You come recommended as a trial attorney, and that's what I expect, if necessary."

Janna was slightly taken aback by her new client's sudden change in demeanor.

"Fine. Understood. If we have to, we'll go to trial then. Now, did you bring me a retainer?"

"Yes. Five thousand, you said?"

"Exactly right."

"Here you are." He handed her a cashier's check for the full amount.

"I will tell you this up front, doctor. Sex cases are difficult through and through. And while it is true that the court's ultimate job is to ferret out the truth, to determine whose story holds more water at a preliminary hearing, the judge will not be assessing the victim's story for its truth. The fact that two of your patients claimed an unwanted sexual act occurred will likely be enough for the judge to find probable cause. So we will probably be looking at a trial.

"Also, unlike the trial process, at the preliminary hearing there is no requirement that the State notify me of whom they plan to call to the stand. But I will still have an opportunity to cross-examine the State's witness, usually one of the victims. It will be the first time the complaining witness will be in a courtroom, confronted by the attorneys, the judge, and yourself. It will be the first time the young woman will have to state the facts aloud and in a public forum. This can be very intimidating and stressful on a victim. I will tread lightly so as not to put off the judge. Understood?"

"Fully."

"Is there anything else I should know right now?"

"Nothing comes to mind."

Janna stood to shake his hand, brushing a strand of her long strawberry blond hair from the corner of her mouth. As she rose from her chair, she could tell Dr. Von Patton was looking at her closely.

Janna was a tall slender woman, attractive in a unique way. One of her large green eyes had a brown spot in its center, for which people often gently teased her, calling it her "cat's-eye." Her face was slightly tanned and splashed with light freckles. She had a wholesome all-American look about her. She was confident in her manner, although seemingly unaware of her own attractiveness. She noticed the doctor looking her over but ignored it. She shook his hand firmly and showed him to the door.

Then she sat back down at her desk to start thinking about possible defenses. It would have to be consent.

The women consented to the anal exams. She turned back to her Westlaw for help, since she wasn't planning to get much from her new client.

She didn't trust him, but that could just be the result of years of training. Never trust a defendant, not even your own client. That was the golden rule.

Chapter Thirteen

Area Four Station
Chicago, Illinois
October 30
10:48 A.M.

Detective Stone drummed his fingers on the small desk, pensively scratching his chin stubble with the other hand. The murders were linked, although the department hadn't made an official statement to the press yet. The patterns among the three victims were consistent. Specifically, the religious symbols found at each crime scene.

The symbols weren't anything satanic or cultlike, quite the contrary, they were simple crosses. The bodies were not horribly desecrated, at least not the ones they had found so far. However, the killer had gotten more aggressive with the third victim. One thing was certain, all the crime scenes shared one common thread: Crosses had been carved into or left in the vicinity of each woman.

The other night, a cross attached to a string necklace had been found wound through the fingers of the dead woman. A cross had also been carved into her stomach. There were three female victims so far. One woman had been clutching a rosary in her hand and the second woman had a cross carved into her hand. All three women had been left with makeshift nooses around their necks. From what he had been told, the knot used to tie the nooses was a Celtic knot, another ancient religious symbol.

What was the killer trying to tell them? What was his message?

As of yet, no one had made a particularly big issue out of the dead women. They were all prostitutes and one also worked as a stripper. They led high-risk lifestyles. They were easy prey. Often women of this type could be missing and it went unnoticed for days. It followed that if no one cared enough to report them missing, generally no one cared that they were missing to begin with.

So far, the TV reporters had only given the news of the recovered bodies three minutes of air time. The papers had been better, printing a front-page story after the discovery of the second body. With the finding of a third corpse things might get shaken up a bit.

Stone felt certain the three deaths were connected,

and it was fair to say the city had an emerging serial killer on its hands. Although he knew the department would try to keep it quiet for a while longer.

Detective Stone continued to drum his fingers on the desk. He had requested a report from the department's forensic profiler. Based on the evidence and the bodies, a profile might assist him in determining what type of person the killer was—where he lived, worked, his personality traits.

So far, there were no witnesses, and Stone needed something to tell him who he should be looking for. Something more than a white male in his thirties, the garden-variety serial killer profile. Detective Stone looked at his Timex, hoping to have the profile by the end of the day.

He leaned forward in his plastic swivel chair, trying to ignore the annoying creaking noise the chair always made. It wouldn't kill the city to invest in some new furniture, he thought. The stuff in the department must have been put in just after the Chicago Fire. It was ancient.

He bit his thumbnail nervously. He needed something to do other than sort through papers. He couldn't just sit here and wait for this guy to kill someone else.

Detective Stone picked up the forensics report on his desk. It was from the first body, a Jane Doe. Prostitute, unknown identity, she had been found in an abandoned building in Chicago's Pilsen neighborhood. The report noted that blue polyester fiber strands had been recovered from the body of the corpse.

The same was true of the second victim, Sharee Nichols. Blue fiber strands were also found on her body. And while he didn't have a report back on the third victim, his guess was that the same blue fiber strands would be recovered from her corpse, if they hadn't been washed away by the flooding in the basement where the killer had dumped her body. The drag marks on the floor and the minimal signs of disturbance told Stone the basement had been only a dumping site, which meant less evidence recovery. And with the extent of the flooding, he would be lucky to get anything back.

Jack Stone heard his partner's telltale whistle out in the hallway.

"Arnie? Is that you?"

"Sure is," Arnie said, coming into the back area of the station, where the desk was. Arnie was Stone's junior and a tall, olive-skinned man. He had a Latin heritage and it often showed in his zest for life.

"Where have you been?" Stone asked.

"I had to go over to my sister's. My niece is sick and my sis had to work. I took the kid to the doctor. Sorry," Arnie offered.

"No problem, you didn't miss anything."

"Nothing new, huh?"

"Not a thing. We have forensics reports back from the first two victims, with fiber analysis. Blue polyester from an unknown source. No control sample." Stone tossed the reports over to his partner. "Have a look for yourself."

"Thanks," Arnie said, taking off his jacket.

"I'm going out for coffee." Jack stood to leave.

"Will you grab me one?"

"First the guy takes the morning off, now you want me to run you coffee?" Stone grinned. The truth was he'd do just about anything for Arnie. The two had been partners for years.

"Extra sugar," Arnie called after Jack, not looking up from the first page of Jane Doe's fiber analysis.

Chapter Fourteen

Pilsen Neighborhood
Chicago, Illinois
November 2—Day of the Dead
1:18 P.M.

Essie grabbed Mariah by her small hand. "Keep up, Mariah. I don't want to lose you."

The thick crowd wouldn't part as people tried to climb to the highest place to watch the colorful flower coronas and paper streamers pass on their way to the cemetery. A man dressed in black with a skeleton's mask danced wildly in the streets to the mariachi band blaring ahead of him. He was waving a long stick with miniature skulls dangling from its end. The music grew louder as the band neared Essie and Mariah, and the crowd tightened as people leaned in to watch the passing parade.

After all, El Dia De Los Muertos came only once a year. The Day of the Dead, a long-honored tradition, called upon Mexicans to pay homage to their dead relatives through a day of festivities and colorful, mocking symbolism. The tradition had found its way to Chicago's Pilsen neighborhood, washing the largely Latin community with a sense of cultural pride and respect for their ancestors. Essie didn't want Mariah to miss the show.

Essie took the day off work and excused Mariah from school. The two left their apartment early that morning to visit the cemetery where Mariah's father was buried. The day had special meaning both in the Latin community and to their small family. Essie had lost her husband more than three years ago, and Mariah her father.

Essie was explaining to her young daughter, "You see Mariah, if we choose to celebrate continued life, if we confront death face-to-face, challenge it, then our remorse and grief can be replaced with belief in a circle of life, the continuance of the soul."

"So Daddy's soul is out there somewhere?"

"Yes, yes it is," Essie answered, believing it herself.

"Is he watching out for us, Mama?"

"With certainty, my little angelita."

The crowd was thickening and Essie was trying to guide Mariah through a narrow opening when her hand slipped out of Essie's and suddenly she heard her shouting from somewhere behind her.

"Mama! Wait, Mama! I can't see you!"

The crowd was taking Essie away from her small daughter. She pressed back toward her, but she was being pushed away too quickly.

"Mariah! Where are you?" Essie yelled.

She had lost sight of her ten-year-old daughter. Panicked, she began to spin around, calling out her name.

The sounds from the mariachi band were blaring in her ears. The Mexican flag colors still trailed before her eyes. She felt sick to her stomach.

"Mariah!"

Another skeleton-man passed by her, rattling his cane in her face, waving his hand at her.

"*Cuidado con la muerte. Ella esta cercas. La muerta vendra por ti!*" he chanted loudly in her face.

Her head was spinning. What was he talking about? He had just told her to beware of death. Death was coming for her? What did he mean by that? The man's gaze penetrated her, boring a hole in her from underneath his mask.

"Mariah!" she screamed again.

The confusion was too much. There were people surrounding her on all sides now. Then she felt someone grabbing her hand.

"Mama! Mama!"

"Mariah!" Essie bent down, holding her daughter in a tight embrace. "You scared me, my angelita! Are you okay?"

"*Sì,*" Mariah replied, wiping tears away from her eyes with her little fists.

81

"Can we go to *abuelita*?" she asked.

"Okay, let's go," Essie agreed.

The two had lost each other for several minutes in the crowd. Essie wasn't about to lose sight of her daughter again. She held on firmly to her wrist, guiding her through the tide of people, as the crowd ebbed on.

The day had been stressful enough for poor Mariah, she thought. That morning the two had visited Joe's gravesite, lighting candles and incense for him. They were on their way to Essie's mother's house for a fiesta-style dinner. Every year her mother would prepare *ceviche*, a *pan de muerto*, stuffed peppers, tacos, and tamales for them.

The distance from the graveyard to her mother's was short, but the parade had proven to be a stubborn obstacle and they were running behind schedule now. Essie didn't want to be too late.

The parade continued to pass. The participants came by in masks, holding up smiling skeletons and waving Mexican flags. Mariah gazed out around the crowd of onlookers and Essie secured her grip on her daughter's hand, guiding her gently through the crowded streets.

She couldn't get the passing parade man's words out of her head though, *Beware of death. It is near.* What did he mean by that?

Essie was more than a little superstitious and if she heard something she generally thought there was a reason for it. She looked down at Mariah and shuddered, hoping the man wasn't talking about the killer lurking in the neighborhood. What bothered her was his last statement, *La Muerta is coming for you.* Maybe Joe was trying to tell her something, to warn her? But of what? She didn't fit the killer's victim type.

Chapter Fifteen

680 North Lake Shore Drive
Chicago, Illinois
November 2
2:28 P.M.

The two had been talking for almost an hour when Dr. Von Patton abruptly announced, "The Xanax isn't working anymore."

"What do you mean it's not working?"

"What I said, it's not working."

"What are you feeling?" the brunette psychiatrist asked. Dr. Lorna Shore was in her late thirties and had been practicing for several years. She was careful with her prescription pad, preferring her patients to work on their issues in session, when possible.

"I'm tense and anxious all the time. I can't seem to

calm myself down. And my seizures have become more frequent, regardless of the Tegretol."

"I see. What's going on at work?"

"I'm still working on the paper for my AIDS research. I need continued funding from NIH if I want to keep the lab open."

"And how's the paper going?" Dr. Shore asked, genuinely concerned for her patient.

"It was going fine, until recently. I haven't been able to work in the last couple of weeks. I'm too worried about this ridiculous court thing." Dr. Von Patton sighed, feeling defeated.

"That's perfectly understandable. The court matter is going to take considerable time and energy, causing you stress over the consequences, whatever the outcome."

"That's just it. I used to be worried about my career path, my reputation in the medical community. Now I'm just hoping I can hold on to my license."

"It does change the perspective on things, that's certain. How is the case coming?"

"Nothing's happening. The preliminary hearing is scheduled for Monday morning, at Twenty-sixth and California. Where I volunteer, for crying out loud. Can you believe it? What luck. I'm going to be standing next to my patients!" Dr. Von Patton almost shouted, frustrated by the thought.

"It's going to be hard for you," Dr. Shore said with empathy.

"Hard? It's humiliating for a man of my stature to have to appear in a criminal court."

"But it won't be the first time," Dr. Shore said gently.

"What are you getting at?" Dr. Von Patton's eyes had narrowed into slits, and he glared at his therapist from his seat on her couch.

"Nothing. I'm just saying you've handled this kind of stress in the past. You can handle it again."

"But this is different. These women were my patients."

"I understand."

"I feel as if the universe is punishing me for something. What could I have done that was so terrible to bring this upon myself? I don't understand." The doctor rested his forehead in the palms of his hands.

"Life can be very difficult at times."

"I've had it with this empathic bull crap," the doctor suddenly snapped. "You're not helping me by agreeing with me on every point."

Dr. Shore moved her chair back slightly from her angry patient, startled by his outburst and his sudden change in tone.

"What do you want to talk about? What would you prefer I say?" she asked quietly, trying to be patient with the obviously struggling man.

"I don't know. I don't care anymore. Just forget it." Dr. Von Patton leaned back into the couch, relaxing once again.

"How about your personal relationships?"

"What personal relationships?" he snorted.

"There must be someone you're involved with? No?"

"No."

"And the urges, the fantasies?"

Dr. Von Patton laughed aloud. "The urges?"

"Yes, are you still having them, the fantasies?"

"About the women you mean?"

"Yes, the fantasies about the women."

"You can't seem to pick a cordial topic for discussion today, can you?"

"That's not why we're here."

"Isn't it? Isn't this therapy just a bunch of semantics, an art form at best? I'm not even sure I believe any of these theories you doctors have."

"You would know as much as I about the accuracy and reliability of modern medicine," Dr. Shore said.

"What kind of fantasies do you have, Dr. Shore? Surely you have certain fantasies as well?"

Lorna Shore shifted uncomfortably in her chair. Her patient was being particularly challenging this morning.

"You know very well I cannot and will not talk about myself in these sessions."

"Well then, I suppose I'll tell you again about my fantasies. If that's what you want to hear about." He grinned sagaciously.

"Only if you like. We can talk about something else, if you prefer." Dr. Shore did not appreciate the insinuation she might want to discuss his sexual perversions for her own gratification. Far from it, she thought.

"The fantasies have stopped. And that's all they were anyway. Just thoughts, fantasies. Everyone has them," the doctor declared loudly.

"Okay."

Dr. Shore changed the subject. "Did you touch these women inappropriately? Your patients?"

"Certainly not. It is entirely unfounded. Even you know I prefer my women a little rough around the edges. These women, my patients, are not my type. Far too stuffy for my liking. Not my preference at all."

"How do you plan to straighten things out, then?"

"That's a very good question. And to be honest, that one I'm going to leave to divine intervention," Dr. Von Patton said.

Dr. Shore looked at her wall clock, then uncrossed her legs and stood.

"Our time is up."

"So it is, my dear doctor, so it is," Dr. Von Patton agreed amicably. "Thank you very much for your time," he said handing her a check. "Now, back to the lab." He stood up and put on his coat.

"Call me if you need anything. And just stay with the Xanax for now."

"You know best. Ta-ta." He tipped his head at Dr. Shore, closing the door behind him, leaving Lorna Shore to wonder exactly what he meant by divine intervention.

Chapter Sixteen

Janna pulled her long strawberry blond hair into a low ponytail. Bent over her notes, she busied herself preparing for her new client's preliminary hearing. Although Janna had done hundreds, this one would be different. She was now a defense attorney, representing the accused, not the State.

She waited in the back of the 26th and California courtroom for the clerk to call her client's name, having informed him that both she and Dr. Von Patton were present and ready to proceed with the hearing.

89

The State would be presenting one witness, one of the alleged victims.

The clerk called the case number and then, "People versus Mason Von Patton."

"Yes, right here." Janna stepped up to the bench and instructed Mason to sit at the defendant's table. She stood before the judge, whom she had known for years.

"Janna Scott for the defendant, your honor."

"Thank you, and for the State?"

"Ian Shea, your honor."

The State's Attorney proceeded with a brief statement of the facts of the case and told the court they were prepared to call their sole witness, one of the victims. Janna had no objections. At the preliminary hearing stage it was unusual and unnecessary for the State to present testimony from multiple victims. Janna seated herself at the defense table next to her client.

"The State calls Kelsey Dore."

A small and timid blond woman in her early twenties at most crossed the courtroom floor and stepped into the witness box. She immediately began to chew on her thumbnail. The State's Attorney let her settle into her seat before beginning his line of questioning.

"Miss Dore, can you state and spell your full name for the record."

"Kelsey Dore. K-E-L-S-E-Y D-O-R-E."

"And your address?"

Kelsey's eyes shifted uncomfortably to Dr. Von Patton and then to Janna. She caught the doctor's eye and immediately glanced down at her fingernails. Fumbling momentarily, she finally responded, "I live at 6218 North Sheridan, Chicago."

"Okay, thank you, Miss Dore. And your age?"

"I'm twenty years old."

The State's Attorney was standing behind a podium, his voice calm and reassuring to his witness, while at the same time lending its strength to her, encouraging her to continue. Janna had to admit the guy seemed to be in control of the courtroom. His confident body language added to his overall "good-guy" image. He first had Kelsey make an in-court identification, pointing out Dr. Von Patton as her doctor. She was now ready to begin her story.

The State's Attorney asked her when she first became a patient of Dr. Von Patton.

"In June of this year."

"And how often did you visit him?"

"Not often. I had been told I might have some kind of exotic bug. I had been feeling ill ever since returning from Belize. I was referred to Dr. Von Patton."

"And did you have an 'exotic bug'?"

"Objection," Janna said loudly. "None of this is relevant to a determination of probable cause for my client's case here, your honor. This woman's health conditions have nothing to do with our purpose for being here today, which is to determine if Dr. Von Patton has any place in this system at all."

The State's Attorney argued, "Your honor, this is necessary foundation and background so we can understand how the victim managed to find herself in Dr. Von Patton's care on the days of the alleged misconduct. We need to know why she was there to evaluate what proper conduct would have been on those visits."

"Overruled," the judge said after a moment's thought. "Proceed, Mr. Shea. But let's get through the testimony this morning if possible," he asked.

"Certainly, your honor. Thank you," the red-haired, freckled State's Attorney replied, turning back to his witness.

"You may continue, Miss Dore. Did you have a 'bug'?"

"They couldn't find anything wrong with me. But several weeks later I became concerned again. I was still experiencing the same symptoms."

"And what symptoms were those?"

"I was fatigued, I was nauseous all the time and suffering from constant diarrhea," Kelsey whispered from the stand.

"Could the witness please speak up?" Janna requested.

"Please speak more loudly, Miss Dore," the judge instructed.

"I was having diarrhea," Kelsey repeated.

"And what did you do?"

"I went back to see Dr. Von Patton."

"When was that?"

"Around July, the same summer."

"And what happened?"

"He offered to do some tests. I told him I suffered

from anxiety in the past, and I asked him if he thought it might be the anxiety, you know, that it had returned."

"Did he do some tests?"

"Yes. He did a blood test, but that didn't show anything."

"I see. And what kind of anxiety did you experience in the past?"

"My stomach was tense, nervous. I felt like I was going to vomit all the time."

"And you were feeling the same nervous stomach when you went to see Dr. Von Patton."

"Yes, something similar."

"And had you ever experienced diarrhea as a result of your nervous stomach?"

"Yes, some."

"Do you drink?"

"No."

"Do you smoke or use marijuana?"

"No, neither."

"Objection. Questions are outside the scope of relevance."

"Sustained. Move on, counsel."

"How was your anxiety treated in the past?"

"I was prescribed Prozac for a brief period of time, but I no longer use anything."

"I see. And when you went to see Dr. Von Patton in June of this year, you believed your symptoms were not from the anxiety but were being caused by some bacteria or rare disease?"

"Objection, leading and calls for medical conclusion by an unqualified witness," Janna said.

"Sustained. Move on, counsel," the judge warned the State's Attorney again, looking at him over the top of his glasses.

"Okay. What happened when you went to see Dr. Von Patton?"

"He told me to put on a gown. I changed while he was out of the room. He came back a few minutes later."

"And then?"

"He examined me briefly. He examined my breasts, my stomach. He felt gently around my hips."

"And did he ask you anything during the exam?"

"Yes, he asked me about my sex life, about sexual intercourse."

"What did he ask?"

"He asked if sex was painful, how often I had sex, how many partners I had. He asked me if I experienced orgasm during intercourse and if my partner provided me with pleasure."

"And did you respond to his questions?"

"Yes. At first they seemed proper. But when he started asking about my orgasms, I became hesitant." Kelsey's voice had dwindled to a whisper. She was looking down at her hands, fidgeting in her seat.

"Please ask the witness to speak up," Janna asked again.

She leaned over to whisper in Dr. Von Patton's ear. "She's practically describing my last physical exam. There's nothing here."

"Then what happened?" the State's Attorney asked.

"Again, I told Dr. Von Patton I suffered from anxiety and asked him if he thought that's what was causing my problems."

"What did he say?"

"He said, no. He thought . . ."

"Objection, hearsay, your honor. The witness is about to restate an out-of-court medical opinion."

"She is explaining what happened. It is not being offered for its medical value, and defense counsel knows it," the State argued.

"Overruled. For now," the judge added.

"What did Dr. Von Patton tell you?"

"He didn't think it was the anxiety. He told me he was going to give me an anal exam."

"And did he do that exam?"

"Yes, on my next visit."

"And did he do anything else?"

"He performed two separate anal exams, on two separate occasions."

"And do you know the purpose for these exams?"

"Objection, your honor!" Janna shouted.

"Sustained. Move on, counsel."

"What happened during the second exam, Miss Dore?"

"The second time . . . he pushed me down on the table. He was, you know, starting to perform the anal exam and he just like, I don't know . . . He pushed me over and then put his finger in, hard."

"How did he push you down?"

"I was laying on my side on the examination table and he pushed me over, rolled me so I was more flat on the table, then he put . . . he jammed his finger in."

"Okay, thank you. Miss Dore, at any time during your exams was a nurse present?"

"No, never."

"Do you have now, or have you ever had an exotic or tropical illness, Miss Dore?"

"No."

"Have you been diagnosed with any illness or disease?"

"Just anxiety."

"Did Dr. Von Patton make this diagnosis?"

"No. It was made by my regular physician."

"No further questions, your honor."

"Thank you. Defense?" The judge motioned to Janna to begin her cross-examination.

Janna rose from her seat, pulling on her gray wool skirt. She sighed audibly, expressing her disapproval for the case. She approached the podium, and stood arrow straight before the court.

"Miss Dore, who referred you to Dr. Von Patton?"

"My doctor at City Memorial. He told me I should see an infectious disease doctor, and he gave me Dr. Von Patton's name."

"Is this the same doctor who diagnosed your anxiety?"

"Yes, but he didn't diagnose my anxiety until after I had seen Dr. Von Patton several times."

"Could the court please instruct the witness to answer only 'yes' or 'no'?" Janna asked the judge.

"Please limit your answers where possible, Miss Dore."

"Miss Dore, when did you first go to the police?"

"I don't recall exactly. A few weeks after the second anal exam."

"You didn't go the police immediately after the first anal exam?"

"No."

"And you didn't go immediately after the second anal exam?"

"No, I really didn't suspect anything at first. It didn't hit me until later that the whole thing seemed kind of odd. I was distraught when I went to see Dr. Von Patton. I really wasn't thinking about his questions or his tests. I just wanted to feel better. I thought maybe I had some kind of rare bug, I didn't know what was wrong with me."

"And even though you say Dr. Von Patton 'pushed' you, you still didn't go to the police right away?"

"No."

"In fact, you returned to see Dr. Von Patton?"

"No. He pushed me the last time I saw him."

"How many visits did you make to Dr. Von Patton?"

"Three total."

"So you kept returning to see Dr. Von Patton, even after you became suspicious of his behavior during your visits?"

"No, that's not what I said."

"You said you returned to Dr. Von Patton for a second anal exam. Even after he had already performed one. Is that correct?"

"Yes," Kelsey answered, defeated.

Janna shook her head with disapproval at the girl's response.

"No more questions, your honor."

"Thank you, counsel," the judge replied.

Janna sat back down, next to a disgruntled Dr. Von Patton.

"That's it? That's what I'm paying you for?" he whispered angrily.

"That's it," Janna whispered back. "You don't take the stand. Not now, and not ever, if I have it my way."

"I don't want to take the stand now. Aren't you going to ask her anything else?" the doctor said a little louder this time.

"Not at a preliminary hearing. I told you that."

The judge interrupted their collusion.

"State, make your argument for my finding of probable cause."

Ian Shea made a brief argument, getting straight to the point.

"Miss Scott?"

Janna stood and argued there was consent by the patient, and that further, the exams were justified due to the nature of the patient's complaints.

"Everyone done?" the judge asked.

"Yes, your honor."

"Okay. I find probable cause exists for this case to remain in the system for the time being." The judge briefly explained his reasoning and dismissed the courtroom personnel, calling a recess.

Dr. Von Patton looked at Kelsey with pure scorn and disgust. Janna, noticing the silent exchange, saw Kelsey look away, visibly upset.

After they exited the courtroom, Dr. Von Patton stopped Janna in the hallway, demanding to know why probable cause was found.

Janna explained to her client, "I told you probable cause is often found. It's a much lower bar to determine probable cause for a case to exist than when a court determines a person's guilt. In other words, all the court is looking at is whether you are the right person charged with the crime and whether the crime you were charged with is the appropriate charge. It's not making any kind of determination on whether you actually committed the crime. That's why it's difficult to get a case thrown out at the preliminary hearing level. At least we established a nice record for trial. I might be able to impeach Miss Dore during trial and she'll lose her credibility."

Dr. Von Patton glared at Janna.

"There's very little I can ask her on the stand during the preliminary hearing, do you understand? My scope is limited to the incident at hand and to help figure out whether the charge should have been brought. We know that you are her doctor and you performed the exams, we can't do anything about that. My only shot was that you shouldn't have been charged to begin with. Basically that she consented and that the exams were reasonable. Just because it didn't work at the preliminary hearing level doesn't mean it won't work at trial. Should there even be a trial. The State has to realize they don't have much here. They're going to be willing to bargain."

"I told you I don't want to bargain anything. I won't accept a plea."

"We don't even know what they're offering."

"I don't care."

"This could ruin your career. You could lose your license. We can get this lowered to battery, eliminate the sexual component entirely. You'll have a better shot of retaining your medical license."

"Doesn't matter. I won't plead guilty to anything, no matter what they lower the charge to or what they offer."

"Fine, then we'll try it."

Dr. Von Patton was rattled, either that or he wasn't as pleasant as he initially wanted Janna to believe. His menacing look warned her he was in no mood for her advice.

"Don't forget which side of the courtroom you sit on now. You're not Marcia Clark, remember?" he hissed at her.

"I certainly won't. That much is for sure," she retorted sharply.

Dr. Von Patton skulked off, mixing in with the

courtroom inhabitants, who were emptying into the hallways of the courthouse. It was the lunch hour.

"This attorney-client relationship is off to a great start," Janna mumbled to herself, stuffing her legal pad into her briefcase.

Chapter Seventeen

Cook County Hospital
Chicago, Illinois
November 6
2:18 P.M.

The strong November sun shone through the barred windows of Cook County Hospital's Jail Section, brightening even the drab walls of the old hospital ward. Looking through the window, one would never know winter was rapidly approaching. The weather in Chicago turned as regularly as a revolving door and that November was no different. In a vast change from the previous month, November started off unusually warm that year. The radiant sunshine dared winter, taunting it to show its gloomy face.

Sarah directed her attention back to her patients,

particularly to James, who was mumbling incoherently. James was no longer comatose. He was coming around slowly. However, even though he had made some progress, he was not yet oriented, and he still didn't respond to human contact or stimulus. His speech had returned slightly, and he would often babble incoherently from his bed.

Today his garbled speech seemed mostly to be about monsters and demons. James was saying something about demons and disease. Sarah moved toward his bed cautiously, not wanting to stop him from speaking.

James's eyes were wide open, boring holes into the ceiling tiles.

"The monster . . . it takes his soul. That's how it gets in, ya know." James paused for a second, then went on with his ramblings. "All diseased. All of them," he slurred. Drool was running down his chin.

Sarah dabbed his mouth with a towel. "Come on now. You're not making any sense to old Sarah."

She adjusted the angle of his bed and made sure he was safely centered on it. The doctor had removed his breathing tube several days ago. James had been breathing on his own and attempting to talk, from wherever his mind was currently dwelling.

"What are you trying to tell me, hmmm . . . ?" Sarah whispered in James's ear as she fluffed the pillow underneath his head.

James had been lying in the same position for hours already. He had barely moved for days. She rolled him over to avoid bedsores.

She knew he would spend the rest of the day staring at the ceiling, drifting in and out of sleep, every once in a while mumbling something or shouting. He never made any sense, though, mostly just jibber-jabber.

Sarah turned on the television hanging from the ceiling at the foot of his bed. Perhaps the movements of the actors would keep him mentally occupied on some subconscious level. Maybe even snap him out of his spell. He had been semi-conscious for more than a week. He couldn't stay in this unit for much longer.

Sarah knew if he didn't come around soon they'd probably wind up moving him to the psych ward at the state mental hospital. Although State was not a pleasant place to be, she knew they wouldn't continue to care for James at Cook County Hospital forever.

One of the other patients called out to Sarah, complaining about pains in his leg. The police had shot him while he was robbing a local White Hen, attempting to feed his heroin habit. He had already experienced several days of painful heroin withdrawal. It seemed he was just about ready to go into another fit.

Sarah walked over to his bedside. "Calm down, just calm down. Sarah's here now," the big black nurse cooed softly to the disturbed patient as she prepared a shot of methadone for the struggling man.

Behind her, James yelped.

"Oh, hold on!" Sarah called. "Just hold on, I'm coming!"

Chapter Eighteen

Area Four Violent Crimes
Chicago, Illinois
November 6
3:42 P.M.

"Hurry up, Arnie. We were supposed to be there ten minutes ago," Jack said to his dawdling partner as he took the stairs two at a time.

"I'm coming, I'm coming," Arnie grunted.

"Cut down on those steak sandwiches and you might be able to keep up." Jack stopped to catch his breath and wait for his partner.

"I'm just tired today, that's all. I couldn't sleep last night. We've been putting in so many hours on this damn case, I think I forgot how."

"I know it. But we don't want them to forget it either. You know how this stuff goes. We'll catch heat if we look like we're not on top of this thing, so let's get into this meeting."

"I hear ya." Arnie caught up to Jack and the two went into an unused conference room in Area Four.

"Val Kramer from Forensic Services. Glad you gentlemen could join us this afternoon," the attractive brunette greeted the two men, while eyeing them accusingly over the top of her tortoise-shell glasses.

"We've been waiting for you both," the commander added, shooting Jack a look.

"Sorry. Arnie got stuck impounding some evidence. We got held up," Jack said.

"Well, sit down. We don't want to waste any more of Ms. Kramer's valuable time. It was nice enough of Forensic Services to send someone over personally."

The Area Four Commander was all politics today, Jack thought.

"Why don't you go ahead and start, Val." The commander nodded at the forensic psychiatrist.

"Okay, gentlemen. We've reviewed what you've sent over—the autopsy reports, medical examiner's report, crime scene descriptions and notes, whatever you had, to try to create some kind of profile for you. This is what we've got."

Val Kramer pulled out a blue folder and handed each of them a neatly typed report on their killer. Jack and Arnie looked it over. For now, they were the only two guys working the case. Apparently, based on the victim profile, the department didn't want to spend any more manpower than needed. A few dead prostitutes, even though it looked serial in nature, didn't require the assembly of a task force in Chicago. At least, not yet.

"Are you going to tell us what this says?" Arnie asked.

"Yes, we can go through the profile summary together. I've provided a more detailed report for your review at a later time." Val turned to page one of her profile, a report on the first victim found.

"First victim, Jane Doe. With her, and for each of the other two victims, I start out with a timeline based on the incident reports provided by your department. The IRs and statements provided give me a general idea of each victim's whereabouts, last time they were seen, that type of thing.

"All three of the victims were last seen sometime in the early evening hours a couple of days before their bodies were found. They all led high-risk lifestyles. If someone did see them in the later hours, it would most likely have been a john, who isn't going to come forward. So it's difficult to pinpoint when exactly these women disappeared."

"So we have no idea is what you're saying?"

"Your department did hand over a couple of statements from people in the neighborhood where these women's bodies were found who claim they saw them in local bars or on the street. Nothing tremendously helpful. The latest sighting on any of the victims is around 7:30 P.M. or so, and that body was found more than twenty-four hours later."

Val let each of the men flip through the report to familiarize themselves with the location of the information she had summarized before continuing.

"All three women were found in abandoned buildings. Two of the bodies were surrounded, almost immersed, in water or flooding. The medical examiner arrived at all three scenes and pronounced the victims dead. This was established from the crime scene notes.

"A review of the autopsy reports showed that the first two victims were asphyxiated. Both received traumatic head injuries prior to their death. Both were found completely nude with rope marks on their ankles. Further, both women appeared to have bite marks on their breasts and inner thighs. Photos were submitted to the forensic odontologist at the crime lab for analysis."

Val paused for a moment, pulling on the chain necklace she was wearing. "As we all know, some type of religious symbol, a rosary, a cross, whatever, was found on or near each woman. And again, from the autopsy on number two and the crime scene notes on number three, it appears that crosses were actually carved into the bodies of the last two victims. No autopsy report back on number three as of yet."

"So what does that all mean? The religious symbolism?"

"I'll get to that. Just let's get through the summary of the facts first."

"Okay."

"Time of death estimate for the first two victims is somewhere in the early hours of the morning approximately forty to forty-five hours before their bodies were found. At best we have a range of two A.M. to seven A.M. This estimate is based on the time of the autopsy, lividity, blanching, and rigormortis analysis. Rigor was present and was fixed to an equal degree in all extremities. It was cold, so rigor would have been slowed, allowing for a couple of days for it to set evenly before decomposition would have started."

She cleared her throat.

"Any questions on the facts so far?"

The three men looked up from their reports, checking each other's reactions.

"No," Jack said.

"Nothing from me," Arnie added.

"Okay, let's continue then."

"Wound pattern analysis. Each victim received multiple abrasions to the head and face. Also, none of the rope marks on these girls' ankles left deep furrows. This indicates that the victims were not struggling while the ligatures were in place. It further indicates that the victims were unconscious when the ligatures were affixed to their ankles, probably knocked out by the blows to their heads. The victims lack defensive wounds, again indicating they were knocked unconscious before they were able to really put up a struggle. Bruising around the neck is consistent with strangulation. Both women we have autopsy reports back on had nooses fastened around their necks. It's believed the ultimate cause of death was asphyxiation by strangulation. However, the nooses may have been tied around their necks after they were already dead."

Val Kramer calmly took a sip of her coffee.

"Next, we're on to the good stuff. Does our guy do this for sexual reasons? It's somewhat iffy, unfortunately. No trace of seminal fluid, no pubic hair, and no indication of forced sexual violation to either of our first two victims. However, bite marks received on the breasts and inner thigh are consistent with heterosexual behavior, and definitely sexual in their nature. The bite marks have angry sexual undertones, based on the bruised and sucking nature of the marks. Based on the violence directed toward these women's faces, their identities, our guy may be impotent, suffering from sexual dysfunction."

"No semen in any of them?" Jack asked.

"Not the first two. However, it is possible semen traces would have been found but were washed away by the flooding. It's unlikely, though. There was no tearing, no abrasions to the vaginal or anal openings. There didn't appear to be penetration."

"What does the lack of penetration mean?"

"Well, among other things, I think the main indication is that our killer is impotent. I also think he's very neat, clean. He doesn't like to leave a mess behind, which is somewhat unusual. No blood. He may even have an aversion to blood, thus the strangulation. Clean and neat this guy likes it."

"But these killings are sexual in nature?"

"Strangulation generally has a sexual undertone. The bite marks also lead me to believe that yes, they are."

"Are we up to the religious symbols yet?"

"Yes, I'm getting to that now. The most important thing is what he is choosing to leave behind . . . the crosses, the rosary. He's trying to send some kind of message. Possibly that he's eradicating or freeing these women's souls. Maybe that they're sinners? That could be too simple. It's too early to be sure what his message is."

"Could it be cult-based?" Jack asked.

"I don't believe so. There aren't any indications that these killings are cult-related. Usually cult-based murder victims are members of the cult itself. The killings are done as a warning to the other members. That's not what's going on here."

"So what's our profile?" Arnie asked.

"I think you're dealing with an educated man, someone who's probably well-organized, neat and tidy. Right now he's going for low-risk victims. People no one will notice missing for a while. To do this he's probably driving a car that won't stand out, something ordinary, that would blend into the neighborhood. Nothing showy. Something large enough to carry a body, though. A four-door sedan type of vehicle."

"What else can you tell us?"

"He's dumping these bodies near or in water, getting rid of most of the trace evidence that would be left behind. He probably knows something about forensic science. He's also gaining these women's trust some-

111

how. No defensive wounds on any of them. They're going with him willingly, at least initially. He could be posing as a john. He could even be in crime prevention. I believe the body location is only the dump site. He attacks them somewhere else and is using his car to transport them."

"You think he might be a cop?"

"I'm not ready to say that. But he's dumping their clothes and leaving them in water. He knows something about crime scene analysis. He's leaving behind only what he wants us to find."

"Like the crosses."

"Exactly."

"So who do we look for?"

"This guy is probably in some type of profession or trade. He has a good knowledge of forensic science. He may be in law enforcement. That may be how he gets his victims to trust him. He may be an authority figure. Probably fairly attractive, a charmer. His skill level is fairly high. He may have been in the system before, past arrests, maybe using an alias if he's in law enforcement. He's either divorced or has never been married. Most likely sexually dysfunctional, he's heterosexual, probably white, mid-thirties. He'll be large, taller. Someone who can overpower these women with some ease."

"Anything else?"

"All serial killers follow certain patterns. Our guy is just finding his. He's a newborn. He probably is establishing his own ritual. He may say something, chant something. They all have rituals. But he's still evolving. The crosses, the nooses—each scene has a little more depth to it. He's finding his niche. And he's definitely becoming more aggressive and more violent with each victim. He actually carved a cross into the bodies of the last two victims."

"Any other questions, fellas?" the commander asked.

"Nah, nothing."

"Okay then. Thank you for your time. And thank you for coming down here personally." The commander stood up from the heavy plastic chair and offered his hand to Val Kramer.

"Just doing my job. You can forward any new reports or new evidence you have to me. I'll be happy to configure any new information into my report."

"Will do," Jack said.

"Good luck to you." She tipped her head at Jack and Arnie before she and the commander exited the conference room.

The commander popped his head back into the room for a brief moment.

"You guys bring me someone in on this soon, got it? The newspapers are going to have a field day with this if it gets out of control." Then he left to escort Officer Kramer out.

Jack sighed.

"You want to start shaking down the other coppers?" Arnie snickered softly.

"No kidding," Jack replied.

Chapter Nineteen

Kelsey felt uneasy. She didn't like the way the doctor had been staring at her in court. He frightened her. Why had she agreed to this? The State's Attorney she talked with encouraged her to come forward, to make sure Dr. Von Patton didn't do this sort of thing again.

Kelsey was happy the judge had found probable cause that morning, but it seemed like there was still such a long road ahead. She didn't know if she could make it through the whole criminal process and then through the trial itself. She had just transferred into Loyola that fall and wanted to get started on the right foot. But this case was already taking a heavy toll on her and her studying, and it was obvious the nightmare was just beginning.

The prosecutor told her Dr. Von Patton had requested a jury. That meant at least a year before they ever saw trial.

She walked up the stairs to her second-floor apartment near Loyola's North Shore Campus. She had just finished with her early childhood psychology class. She glanced back over her shoulder before unlocking the apartment door.

This whole experience had really shaken her, and lately she always felt like someone was following her, watching her. A chill ran down her spine and she shuddered.

Kelsey was afraid the doctor was going to come after her. He was an intimidating man, and he had already done her enough harm. She just wanted to move on with her life.

Why had she agreed to come forward? Why didn't they have the other woman testify this morning? Why her?

She walked into the apartment and instantly relaxed when she saw her boyfriend, Jeff, sitting on the couch watching television while eating a bowl of cereal.

"Hey, sweetie," she greeted him.

"Hey, baby. How was class?"

"Dull, to be quite honest." She dropped her book bag on the floor near the doorway.

She bolted the door behind her and peered out the

peephole into the hallway, just to make sure no one was out there.

"You okay, Kelsey?" Jeff asked.

"Yeah, I'm just worried, shaken up still, I guess."

"About this court stuff?"

"Bingo. And Jeff Wolcott gets the grand prize," she said sarcastically, curling up next to him on the couch.

"How'd court go this morning?"

"I hated every minute of it. Why do I have to keep telling this story over and over? It's like I'm forced to relive the whole ordeal every time. They won't let me forget."

"Who won't?"

"The dumb attorneys, the cops, all of them."

"They're just trying to get this guy. You have to be strong. I'm here for you. You know that, whenever you need someone."

Kelsey twirled a piece of long blond hair around the tip of her index finger, examining the strands for split ends under the overhead light.

"It's the way he was looking at me this morning. In court no less! I mean, my God, does this man have no shame? He's just so creepy, so invasive." She shivered noticeably.

"I knew I should have gone with you today."

"No really, you didn't need to. You had a test."

"What can I do?" Jeff asked her.

Kelsey knew he felt helpless even though he was a criminal justice major and would have done just about anything for her.

"I just don't think I can go through with this whole thing. I can't do it."

"I don't blame you. I know it has to be brutal. If you really don't think you can handle it, tell them you won't testify."

"They'll subpoena me, and I can be charged criminally if I don't show up."

"Who told you that?"

"One of the lawyers."

"That's a bunch of crap. They're just messing with your head, that's all."

"I don't think so. I think it's true."

"Why don't we call a lawyer of our own?" Jeff suggested.

"With what money?" Kelsey snorted. "All that big cash I made working at the deli last summer?"

"I've got some money I could lend you."

Kelsey stretched and rose from the couch. "No, but thank you. I really do appreciate the offer." She walked into the apartment's little kitchen to make herself something to eat.

She was glad Jeff was over and didn't want him to leave.

Just then someone knocked at her door. Kelsey walked over and checked the peephole. It was a pizza man. She opened the door.

"Can I help you?" she asked, confused as to why the pizza deliveryman was on her doorstep.

"Did you order a pizza, Jeff?"

"Nope, sure didn't."

"Kelsey Dore?" the deliveryman asked.

"Yes, but we—"

"You've just been served." The deliveryman handed her an envelope and walked away. Kelsey stood stunned in the doorway, staring after him.

"A lawsuit?" she finally asked. But the deliveryman was long gone.

Book III

The Soldier

Chapter Twenty

The man seemed nice enough, Tara thought. She didn't usually leave with strangers, but something told her she would be safe with this man. She trusted him. Besides, he had told her he was a Chicago police officer, a former evidence technician turned detective. How much safer could it get?

She drained the rest of her beer from the pint glass. The band had started to wind down, and she figured they'd be calling "last round" soon. She took a small compact out of her purse and checked her eye makeup.

Good enough. She was just drunk enough not to care what she looked like anyway.

Tara walked over to the detective, who was standing near the back of the room.

"Music is too loud," he shouted, pointing to his ear.

. The two had been talking for over an hour. Tara, a hair stylist, had been having troubles with her boy-friend. She just discovered he had been lying to her for months, telling her he was divorced. As it turned out, Tara learned that not only was he still married, he hadn't even filed for a divorce. Jerk.

But now it was her turn to get even. And to get some attention for herself, which she certainly needed. This detective seemed to want to give her plenty of that.

She tossed her hair back over her shoulder and flashed a big, toothy grin at the detective. Tara knew she was a knockout.

He was older than she usually preferred, but who cared? She wasn't marrying the guy.

"Do you want to get out of here?" she asked with a mischievous look on her face.

"Is that a question or an invitation?"

"What do you think?"

"I think I'm with you," he replied, resting his Jack Daniels and Coke on the sidebar.

"Great, let's blow this pop stand," Tara yelled, lead-ing the way out.

Not long after they left the bar, they were in the front seat of his car. He was groping her breasts, reach-ing his hand down between her legs.

Tara's skirt was riding up on her thighs, and she groaned audibly as the guy grabbed her inner thigh.

"You want me to go down on you?" he asked.

"Here? We're on the street!"

"It's okay. It's a side street and a dead-end. No one's going to come down here."

"Why don't we just go back to my place?" she suggested.

"I don't think I can wait that long." He grabbed her hips and pulled her legs up onto the bench seat.

Tara shrieked with delight. This was exactly what she needed. Screw her old flame. He was as good as forgotten. Who cared about some old married man?

Her new friend had his face buried between her legs and was kissing and sucking on her inner thigh.

"Don't stop, whatever you do," Tara moaned.

"Not a chance. Don't worry about that. You're going straight to heaven tonight," the cop said, reaching up behind him to lock the car doors.

"Straight to heaven! Express!" Tara yelled in glee, reeling from the effects of the alcohol and the hormones that were raging through her body. She hadn't felt this good in months.

Chapter Twenty-one

Beaubien Woods
Cook County, Illinois
November 7
4:13 A.M.

The Soldier gazed up at the night sky, the stars twinkling dimly, trying to shine from beneath the factory haze that had blown across the lake from Gary, Indiana. The killer howled up at the full moon. It didn't matter. No one was in the woods at this time of night. He knew he was safe.

The thick forest blanketed him from the sounds of I-94, not that many travelers had been on the highway when he made the drive down from the north side.

The weather had turned cool again, and a harsh wind blew through the open area of the woods. The

Soldier crouched near the edge of the Calumet River, trailing his fingertips in the icy water. He could see his shadow on the water's surface. The water looked calm, the moonlight reflecting off the few ripples that disturbed the otherwise glassy top. It would make a good resting place for her body. The water would help cleanse the woman's tainted soul.

The Soldier thought about it for a minute. The barges that came up and down the river would eventually tear the girl's body apart, leaving no evidence for the pesky cops. However, if the barges didn't come by soon, her body would float up and be discovered early. He didn't have anything to weigh her down with.

He heaved the plastic garbage bag up from the ground and peeked inside at the hair stylist's broken body, lying twisted and mangled inside. He bent down to smell her hair once more. Then he closed the top and thrust the bag down toward the river's edge. The top of the bag opened slightly and water began to seep in as the river lapped at the land. He placed a heavy rock from nearby on the bottom of the bag, hoping to hold the girl's body in its place for a few days. He didn't want her discovered for a while.

If no one found the corpse within the next few weeks, it would be too late to catch him. The area would soon be blanketed with snow and it would be spring before anyone found her decomposed remains. That would be ideal.

The Soldier glanced furtively over each of his shoulders. It was after 4:00 A.M. on a weekday morning. No one would be out here, especially not on this cold November morning.

The killer crossed himself and bent his head in silent prayer for the dead girl. He murmured a few lines from the Hail Mary. Then he walked briskly away from the dumping site. It was late. He needed to get home. He had to work tomorrow.

As he ran through the woods, a branch hit him in the face, scratching him right above his eyelid. He yelped, more out of surprise than pain. He reached up to cover the sting with his hand.

That bitch, he swore under his breath. This was all her fault. He hadn't meant to kill the woman at first. She was not one of The Intended, not part of his plan. But then again, it wasn't his plan. It was God's plan. And apparently, God had something else in store for the young woman. And he was God's Soldier of Death, here to do the Lord's work.

The hair stylist had pushed him to the brink, to the edge. She wouldn't let up, even though he had tried to push her off him. She had asked for his vengeance, brought it upon herself.

The woman seemed so surprised when he had grabbed her by the throat. She had struggled at first, clawing at his face, tearing at his hair. She had grabbed at his clothes. But he was far stronger than the small woman, and he had won. He thought about her face again.

Her eyes were pools of fear, her voice gurgling as he stole her last breath. She had been shocked. Then he had kissed her dead lips, still warm beneath his, holding her and rocking her lifeless body. He wanted to apologize to her.

But he couldn't apologize for God. He couldn't do anything about the girl's fate. The Soldier of Death was nothing more than a messenger, sent directly from above. He had to remember his purpose and not allow his emotions to get in the way. He was the Chosen One. And if he didn't follow through with instructions, if he failed, he knew he himself would meet God's wrath.

Chapter Twenty-two

Pilsen Neighborhood
Chicago, Illinois
November 7
1:12 P.M.

Essie wondered why the lady lawyer was calling her. Could it possibly have something to do with her late husband's financial affairs? Although Joe had been a good man and a kind husband, he was not particularly organized when it came to his personal affairs, and his debts haunted Essie for a long time after his passing. She had spent months cleaning up bills and trying to collect on various life insurance policies held through his past employers. It had taken her quite a while to sort through all his scattered papers.

Even so, she had missed a creditor or two. Perhaps

this attorney wanted money from her. That was one thing Essie definitely did not have. After paying off Joe's debts and the rest of her car loan, she didn't have much left over from the life insurance benefits. And with Mariah and the cost of the baby-sitters, things had gotten more than a little tight.

But hiding wouldn't do her any good; she had learned that much. She decided to call the attorney back. Unlike her late husband, she preferred to clear things up as soon as possible, even debt.

She looked again at the message Mariah had scrawled in her childish handwriting. It was barely legible. Where had the sitter been when the phone rang, she wondered?

Essie dialed the number and waited for someone to answer. It only took a couple of rings.

"Janna Scott, can I help you?"

"This is Esmerelda Ruiz, or Essie Ruiz. I'm returning your call."

Janna leaned back in her chair. Finally, the woman was calling her back. Janna received Esmeralda Ruiz's name from Dr. Von Patton as someone who might be a potential character witness for him during trial. Essie was a nurse who worked with Dr. Von Patton at the hospital on occasion. Dr. Von Patton had told Janna that Ms. Ruiz was aware of his character, as well as his volunteer and community work.

Although Janna was seasoned enough to know that using character evidence was usually a bad idea, she was leaving the possibility open in this case. Using character evidence could open the door for the prosecution to retaliate with negative testimony. If she chose not to introduce character evidence, the State couldn't either. However, Dr. Von Patton had told her he didn't have a criminal background, so there shouldn't be much the prosecutor could use against him.

After some thought, she decided it might not be a bad idea to have a witness prepped who could testify to Dr. Von Patton's professionalism and his volunteer work with patients.

Talking with some of the staff would also help her determine if the State had contacted anyone in the hospital, perhaps in an effort to gain negative testimony about Dr. Von Patton's work actions.

Even if Janna didn't introduce evidence about Dr. Von Patton's character, the State could still try to introduce negative character testimony about Mason Von Patton by arguing that it was being introduced to establish a pattern, or to show the doctor's habits.

Janna knew she had to be careful here. She sighed and began her interview of Essie Ruiz.

"Ms. Ruiz, my name is Janna Scott. I'm an attorney, and I've been hired by Dr. Mason Von Patton. You work with him at Cook County Hospital, right?"

Essie hesitated before replying, "Yes, I do."

"There's no reason to be alarmed or concerned. I promise you my call has nothing to do with you or your work. I'm only calling on behalf of Dr. Von Patton. I'm representing him on some matters and would like to ask you a couple of questions. He suggested you might be familiar with his work habits."

"His work habits? I don't know anything about his work habits," Essie stammered, apparently not trusting Janna.

She approached the topic from a different angle. "Have you worked with Dr. Von Patton?"

"Yes, I work with him sometimes at Cook County Hospital. He has privileges there."

"Can you just tell me what your thoughts are on his work, his attitude toward patients, that sort of thing?"

"Dr. Von Patton is a very good doctor, excellent. He is also a very nice man. I don't have anything bad to say about him, Ms. Scott," Essie said defensively.

Janna rolled her pen with the palm of her hand back and forth across her desktop. "I'm not asking you to say something bad about him, quite the contrary. I'm representing him, do you understand?"

"Yes, I understand. Is he in some kind of trouble?"

Janna ignored the woman's question, continuing on with one of her own. "Do you enjoy working with Dr. Von Patton?"

"Yes. He's always considerate of the hospital staff, never condescends to the nurses. He's a nice guy, very hard-working."

"Do you know about his volunteer work?"

"A little. I know he volunteers over at the jail. That's sometimes why he's over at the hospital. Sometimes he'll have a patient by us. He lectures and stuff like that, I know."

"Do you like Dr. Von Patton as a person?" Janna finally asked.

"I guess so," Essie replied slowly, always cautious of lawyers. "Why so many questions?"

"At this time I really don't have any more information for you, Ms. Ruiz. I can tell you we may need your testimony at some later date, just as to your opinion of the doctor's work, his character."

"Testimony?" Essie asked, clearly not happy with where the conversation was headed.

"Nothing is certain at this time. I just wanted to talk to you and get some information."

Some information about my own client, Janna thought. This case was going nowhere fast.

"Okay. Well, is that it?"

"For now, yes. But I may need to call you again in a few months. Would that be all right? Would you be willing to testify on Dr. Von Patton's behalf?"

"I suppose so," Essie agreed reluctantly.

"Thank you, Ms. Ruiz."

Janna gave her phone number to the woman again and told her to call if she had any questions regarding their conversation.

She hung up the phone, somewhat relieved. At least the woman hadn't said she hated Janna's client, or that he was an arrogant pompous ass.

She could get Essie Ruiz to testify if she needed her. For now, that was all that mattered.

Chapter Twenty-three

Loyola University, North Shore Campus
Rogers Park, Chicago
November 7
8:32 P.M.

Kelsey's class had been dismissed a few minutes early, which didn't bother her in the least. She ran down the stairs of Cudahy Hall and started her walk home. She tucked her chin into her turtleneck and bent her head toward her chest, trying to protect her skin from the harsh lake winds blowing across the lakefront campus. She listened to the crunch of the fallen leaves under her Skechers shoes.

Kelsey couldn't concentrate anyway, so an early dismissal was just what she needed. She couldn't keep her mind off stupid Dr. Von Patton. The jerk was actually suing her. She had been served with a summons to appear and file an answer to a civil lawsuit for defamation of character, or slander. Now she would have to hire a lawyer. She felt exasperated and overwhelmed by the whole situation.

This wasn't what she had in mind when she had gone to the police in the first place. She had only wanted to report Dr. Von Patton, so if he hurt anyone else the police would realize he had done this before. Or something like that.

Unfortunately for her, it turned out she was the second victim to report misconduct by the doctor that month, and the police had charged Dr. Von Patton. Kelsey didn't know how this thing had gotten so out of hand. It had blown up in her face.

She picked up her pace, cutting across the campus drive so she could make her way out to Sheridan Road. She slipped past the electronic gate-arm at the campus' edge. That was when she noticed the car.

Its headlights were right on her as she exited the campus. It looked like some kind of Mercedes or something, an older car. She squinted into the car's headlights, shielding her eyes. She couldn't make out the driver.

She quickened her pace, eager to get home. She hoped Jeff would come over and hang out with her. She walked rapidly down Loyola Avenue toward Sheridan Road, but the car didn't pass her. It stayed behind, following her.

She glanced back over her shoulder, a new habit she had formed. The car had its brights on and she couldn't see anything.

She rounded the corner onto Sheridan Road. The car was still behind her. Almost running, she arrived at her walk-up apartment building and called the police as soon as she was safely inside.

Thankfully, someone spoke with her right away.

"Did you see the person following you?" the officer who answered her call asked.

"No."

"What kind of car was this person driving?"

"I'm not sure, I think some sort of Mercedes or something."

"Are you sure it was a Mercedes?"

"No."

"Do you know what color the car was?"

"It was a dark color, like blue or black, but I guess I can't be sure."

"Did you get a license plate number?"

"No, I didn't." Kelsey sighed, sensing the outcome of the phone conversation.

"There's not much we can do to help you if you can't give us some basic information, miss."

"I'm telling you a man was following me tonight and I know exactly who it is!"

"I realize you're upset, but without a basic description, and if he didn't make any contact with you . . . there really is nothing we can do. I'm sorry."

"Fine!" Kelsey slammed the phone down, frustrated

more with herself for not seeing anything than she was with the police for not helping her.

She knew it was Dr. Von Patton. He was trying to intimidate her, to scare her out of testifying.

She hated to admit it, but it was working.

Chapter Twenty-four

West Lake Street, West Chicago Loop
November 8
3:18 A.M.

The Soldier of Death just had been out the previous night. He knew he had to be careful, not let himself get out of control, but the pressure was mounting. He needed to go out, to be in the nightlife, surrounded by the personalities that came into existence only after the rest of the city was fast asleep. The energy he had at night was entirely different from his energy during the day. The Soldier of Death thrived at night, enveloped by the cool and dark night air. That was when he came alive.

He hadn't expected for it to feel so good, so right, when he killed the hair stylist. Until then, his prey had been limited to prostitutes, but obviously he was ready for greater challenges. He was God's Soldier and he would be God's messenger.

He cruised through a couple of bars, a club or two, but nothing seemed interesting. Nothing was jumping out at him. Could it be there was no assignment for him tonight? There had to be. In a city filled with sinners, he knew it was only a question of time before his next task was made known. And he needed to appease his master, for he already knew what happened when he did not obey God's command.

The Soldier went into a trendy new nightclub. There he found a young kid selling Roofies. A popular club drug, sometimes known as the date-rape drug, its active ingredient was Rohypnol. The drug could be easily slipped into someone's drink and, once ingested, caused memory loss and even unconsciousness. It was easy enough to get in the clubs, selling for as little as five dollars per dose. The Soldier bought six doses.

He pocketed the Rohypnol tablets and stayed at the club for another hour, slamming down a couple of drinks and feeling the music pulsating, vibrating through his body. He had an idea.

He decided to go to the Ram's Head Tavern to look for the girl. He had first seen her a couple of months ago. He had followed her, learned where she lived and where her favorite hangouts were. He knew she went to Nick's on weekends, and he had visited the local tavern several times to watch her. On one occasion, he had even spoken to her. He knew his face would be familiar to her by now, a friendly face, one she would vaguely recognize.

Initially, he hadn't known why he was following the girl, but now that he had killed the hair stylist, it had become clear. It was part of God's Plan. She too, was one of the Intended. It was time for him to have higher ambitions, to abandon the street women.

The Soldier knew the girl often went to the Ram's Head Tavern after working an all-night shift. The Ram's Head was a local bar frequented by tourists and newspaper reporters. Because so many of its customers worked nights, the doors opened at 6:00 A.M. Excited by the prospect of finally being face to face with her, the soldier lingered in the caverns beneath Michigan Avenue, counting the minutes until he would have her.

No one would recognize him at the Ram's Head. He was not a regular there. He would remain just another nameless face in the crowd, a no one.

He had dressed in plain clothes that evening, not wanting to stand out. Wearing a pair of blue jeans and a tan barn jacket, he had left some stubble on his chin and thrown on a baseball hat, pulling the lid down over his eyebrows.

The Soldier breezed quietly into the Ram's Head and slowly approached the bar. He took a seat in a dark corner, where he would remain inconspicuous.

She was seated only two seats away, on her usual stool.

* * *

Jordan Nash had just gotten off work. A crime journalist with the *Tribune*, she hung out at the Ram's Head on lower Michigan, as did several of the other reporters. Reporters would often sit at the bar until nearly noon, drinking heartily after a night of hard work.

Jordan, armed with her usual Bloody Mary, didn't even notice the man at the far end of the bar until he slid up next to her and spoke.

"Hey, I know this sounds corny, but you look familiar to me."

Jordan looked closely at him. "You're right, it does sound corny, but the truth of it is, I think I do know you from somewhere." She squinted, trying to place his face. "I'm a crime journalist, and I usually don't forget a face."

The man leaned in toward her, seemingly interested in what she was saying. "Really? I'm a homicide detective. Maybe we worked together."

"No, that's not it. You hang out at Nick's sometimes, don't you?" Jordan finally guessed.

"Yeah, I do. I live over there. How about you?"

"That's where I know you from! I knew I'd figure it out."

The two chatted amicably for a few minutes, and then Jordan ordered herself another Bloody Mary. She was starting to enjoy the man's company. One of her fellow reporters waved goodbye to her on his way out.

"Have a good one, Jimmy!" she called out, then turned her attention back to her new companion.

The detective was talking to her about the importance of protecting a crime scene, photographing it immediately, and preserving the evidence.

Jordan listened intently for several minutes before admitting to the detective she was growing tired of crime reporting and thinking of doing something different with her life.

"Really?" the detective asked, surprised.

"Yeah, I'm just . . . I don't know, my heart's not in it anymore."

"That's too bad."

"You know what? I have to use the ladies' room."

As she turned away, her new friend slyly slipped a crushed Roofie into her Bloody Mary. Jordan didn't see it.

She reappeared from the restroom and hopped up onto the barstool. "I'm exhausted," she announced. "I think I need to go home and get some sleep."

"I don't blame you. I know the feeling." The detective laughed. "Crime is a tiring business."

Jordan gulped down the rest of her Bloody Mary, explaining to the detective, "It helps me sleep."

He smiled at her. "I'm sure it will."

Within several minutes of her last swallow, her head started to get fuzzy. Her vision became blurred, and she felt extremely light-headed.

"I don't feel so great," she said.

"Why don't you let me take you home?"

"Okay," Jordan readily agreed. "Goodnight, Sal," she said to the bartender.

" 'Night, Jordan," the burly man replied. "Looks like you had one to many, huh?"

"I think so. Tough night." Jordan's speech was slurred and she was losing her coordination.

The detective helped her off the barstool and led her out to his car.

Chapter Twenty-five

26th Street and California Avenue
Criminal Court Building
November 8
9:07 A.M.

Janna walked into the main building after visiting with one of her criminal clients, a drug dealer in Division Seven. She stopped in the hallway that connected the administration building to the courthouse. Janna sorted through the files in her shoulder bag, making sure she had the bond release form her client had signed. She found the form and pulled it out. She needed to go to the clerk's office on the fifth floor to file it.

She hoisted her bag up on her shoulder and started walking toward the elevator bank on the administrative side. The center hallway connecting the two halves of the county building was made of pure glass, with two huge center glass doors serving as the only entryway to both buildings. Civilians had already begun to pour through the doors and were waiting in long lines to go through the metal detectors, the only thing keeping them from the loved ones who awaited them in their respective courtrooms.

Janna maneuvered through the crowded hallway and noticed the news reporters setting up their cameras. The Harding case was set for a pre-trial hearing that morning, she remembered. A prominent theater owner's ex-wife had attempted to have him killed. The city news reporters were all over the story, which promised a nice mixture of local celebrity and scandal, a sure seller.

When Janna got to the elevator banks there was already a huge crowd. Two of the six elevators had been reserved to transport jurors from the second floor. The remaining four elevators were taking their time getting down to the ground floor. Janna exhaled loudly.

"When are they going to get these things fixed?" she asked a nearby sheriff.

"Your guess is as good as mine. They put these things in around the same time they put in that lovely orange carpeting upstairs. I think they're waiting for them to become antiques and accrue some value," the sheriff joked.

Janna chuckled.

"Hey, counselor," she heard someone say from behind her.

She leaned back to see where the familiar voice was coming from.

"Hey, Miss Scott."

Janna caught Detective Jack Stone's eye and realized he was the one who had been calling her name.

"Hi there, detective."

"What are you doing back in this place? I heard you moved on to bigger and better things."

Janna laughed. "I moved on all right, but the same people. Just the other side."

"No kidding? You're a defense attorney now?"

"You got it."

"I can't believe you're representing this scum," the detective said, waving his arm toward the people still coming into the front hallway.

"Be nice. This scum is paying my bills. I went into private practice—for myself. I've got to do something to keep my lights on."

"I never figured you for a sellout, Janna," Detective Stone gently teased.

"I'm not a sellout, I promise. Just a couple criminals so I can afford my heating bill this winter. I hear the gas bills are going to be awful." She grinned at him. "Besides, with you on the streets, these guys don't have a chance. They'll be back in before they even get to Ogden Avenue. If there's one thing I've found I can count on, it's the recidivism rate for our loyal offenders. Never a shortage of repeat customers."

"Yeah, no kidding. They must like it here or something," Stone agreed.

"I guess. It can't be the food."

"I hope not. Not if it's the same stuff they're serving in the cafeteria."

"Hey, have you heard anything about a Dr. Mason Von Patton?" Janna asked, changing the subject.

"I read something about it in the papers the other day, but nothing around the shop. He one of yours?"

"Sure is. I just wondered if maybe you knew the arresting officer."

"Where was he arrested?"

"In front of his house, on Indiana."

"Brought to Central?"

"Yup."

"Nah, I wouldn't know him. I work out of Area Four now, Violent Crimes. Hardly know any of the new guys down at Central."

An elevator arrived and several people pushed their way on, leaving Stone and Janna to wait a little longer.

"This is ridiculous," Janna said, glancing at her watch.

"What do you expect from the county?"

"I suppose I shouldn't expect much, huh?"

Detective Stone looked over at Janna and tugged on his shirt collar.

"I know this is kind of impromptu. I don't really see you much anymore, but . . ."

Janna knew what was coming next. She and Stone had known one another for years, but only in a professional way. Although she had sensed his attraction to her, she had never acted on it. Stone was visibly tense.

She tried to make him laugh, to loosen him up a bit, or maybe to change the subject, she wasn't sure.

"Hey, don't be so sure you won't be seeing me around. I might be cross-examining you one of these days," she joked.

He laughed. "I look forward to it, counselor."

The elevator call button rang.

"Would you want to go out sometime?" Stone asked quickly as she stepped into the elevator.

"I'd love to. Call me, I'm listed," Janna said just before the elevator doors closed.

"I will."

Chapter Twenty-six

Somewhere in South Chicago, Illinois
November 8
3:28 P.M.

Jordan opened her eyes slowly. Her eyelids felt as if they had been taped shut, but it was just eye crust. She blinked a few times. Her vision was awfully blurry and her head was pounding as if she had spent the previous night at a rock concert. Had she?

Where was she?

She rolled over, her body aching, and realized she was in the backseat of a car. She tried to sit up, but her body wasn't listening to her mind. Jordan coughed a couple of times. She felt horrible. What had happened to her?

She vaguely remembered going to the Ram's Head

after work. She hadn't gotten there until around 7:30 in the morning or so. What time was it now? She glanced down at her wrist and noticed her watch was gone. That was odd. She must have lost it.

Even stranger, though, was that she was lying wrapped in a blanket in the backseat of some unknown car. Jordan strained to remember anything, but couldn't. Something told her she didn't want to be in this car, though.

She tried to pick her head up. This time her body responded. She craned her neck and managed to peer out the car window. She didn't recognize anything. Where was she?

She tried to move her legs, but they wouldn't budge. She looked down at her feet and saw that they were bound.

What was going on?

Jordan was starting to panic.

Stay calm.

Just stay calm.

She leaned sideways in the backseat and started pulling on the rope around her ankles. It wasn't bound very tightly and she was able to loosen the cords fairly easily. She knew she had to get out of this car.

She tried to pull herself up with her arms. This time her body worked. She lifted her torso up enough to get a better look out the car window. She still didn't recognize anything. Where the hell was she?

Jordan shook her legs and realized they had fallen asleep. Pain shot through her calves and thighs as she tried to revive them. The blood began to pulse through her veins and it felt as if a thousand needles were pricking her simultaneously. She knew she needed to get out of the car *now*. She rolled herself completely over and sat up.

She tried the door. It was locked. She tugged on the metal lock button but couldn't raise it. She was starting to sweat and felt like she was going to throw up. Her body fell forward and her stomach lurched. She could taste the acid in the back of her throat. Then, she vomited all over the car floor.

Damnit.

She closed her eyes tightly and willed her body to start responding.

Everything seemed like it was in slow motion. Finally, she heaved herself into the front seat. She noticed the car's interior. Was she in a police car? She couldn't tell. She couldn't remember anything.

Jordan looked down at the ignition. No keys. The doors were all locked.

Shit.

Why couldn't she get them open?

She leaned back on the bench-style front seat and kicked at the driver's side window with her heel as hard as she could. Nothing. She tried again. This time she heard the crackle of glass splintering and felt the window give under the force of her kick. Cracks exploded from the impact point like a spider's web tracing through the window.

Once more. Just once more. That's all she needed. She kicked again. The glass shattered.

Okay, she told herself. Almost there.

She wrapped her fists in the blanket she had been covered with and started punching the remaining shards out of the window frame. Once the frame was clear enough, she lunged through the frame and fell to the ground. Picking herself up, Jordan started to run.

A few feet from the car, her legs still numb, her foot caught on a crack in the asphalt and she tripped. She landed hard on her hands, bending her wrists back. The palms of her hands stung and were bleeding. She managed to stand up again, though, and kept running. Behind her, she heard someone yelling.

"Hey! Wait up! Where are you going?"

The voice sounded familiar, and thankfully it also sounded far away. She didn't look back to check. She kept running, willing her legs to run faster.

As she ran from the car, she noticed she was in some sort of abandoned parking lot. There were cracks all over the pavement. Her head was spinning and everything was blurry, but she kept going.

From behind, she could still hear a man yelling, angry, telling her to stop.

Up ahead, through some trees, Jordan could see a road with cars passing. She burst into the trees, branches swatting her cheeks. Holding her arms in front of her face to protect herself, she ran through the strip of forest out onto an avenue of some sort. She had stumbled onto a fairly major road. A car honked loudly and swerved, barely missing her.

Reaching up for her throat, she realized a rope was tied loosely around her neck still. She began to wave her arms frantically.

Tears began to stream down her face, but she had no idea why. Her body ached all over. Cars were passing frequently. She continued to wave her arms, until a car finally stopped.

The kind lady who stopped to pick up Jordan drove her straight to the nearest police station. Dirty and sobbing, Jordan reported that she had been drugged and kidnapped.

Now, she had been sitting at the police station for two hours and had already spoken with three police officers, but she still couldn't remember anything significant about her attacker.

Officer Lisa Timpson was giving it one last effort.

"You were at the Ram's Head Tavern earlier this morning, right?"

"That's right," Jordan told the young officer.

"And you were talking to a man at the bar?"

"Yes. I had seen him before. I knew him somehow. I can't remember from where though."

"Okay, do you remember what he did?"

"Umm . . ." Jordan visibly strained herself trying to remember anything from the previous several hours. "I think he told me he was a cop. A detective."

"A cop? One of ours? CPD?"

"I think so. I can hardly remember . . . he must have slipped something into my drink. I don't remember anything after my last Bloody Mary."

"That much makes sense."

Earlier, Timpson noticed Jordan's wrinkled white oxford was covered in gray and blue fuzz. She called an evidence technician to the station. When Officer Lewis arrived, Officer Timpson brought him to the private room where Jordan was waiting. Jordan could hear their voices outside the door.

"This is the victim right in here." Officer Timpson motioned Lewis into the small room.

"I took the rope from around her neck. It's in the bag." Officer Timpson handed the technician a brown paper bag.

Officer Lewis came into the room and introduced himself. He had a kind, soft face. He looked Jordan over from head to toe. "You're going to need to give me your shirt. It has fiber strands all over it. I have something you can change into," he told Jordan.

"I'm going to take a couple of fiber samples right here before she moves too far," he said to Officer Timpson.

The technician offered Jordan a t-shirt. He left her alone momentarily so she could remove her oxford and pull the t-shirt on. When he returned, Jordan gave him her oxford and watched as he removed some of the gray wool fibers with a pair of tweezers and put them in a glass vial. She noticed him sticking something to the oxford she had just been wearing.

"What's that?" Jordan asked.

"Tape."

"For what?"

"I'm taking your shirt with me, but I'm taping it first, to pick up fibers I can't see. Just to make sure they're not destroyed. I'm going to take all of it to the crime lab for analysis."

"You're kidding, right?"

"Nope. This is the only link we have between you and the offender right now."

"You take the sample with tape?"

"Yup. Pretty high-tech stuff, huh?"

"No kidding. You think I would know this stuff as a crime journalist."

"Not necessarily. You report the crimes, right? You're not writing about how evidence is analyzed."

"I guess," Jordan agreed half-heartedly, not really convinced but enjoying how sweet the technician was acting toward her.

When he finished, he left the room. Officer Timpson wanted to talk to her further.

"I'm going to give you my card. If you remember anything else later today, anything at all, please call me. No pressure. Just take your time, something might come back to you. I'm going to have to fill out a report and submit it today. Your case will be assigned to a detective from the area, and someone will contact you soon, okay?"

Jordan's head was in her hands. She couldn't believe any of this was happening to her. It was all so surreal.

She felt as if she had been transposed into a Salvador Dali painting.

"Is that it?" she asked, taking the card from the officer.

"Yeah, but like I said, no pressure. Call me if you remember anything else in the next day or so."

"I will. Can someone take me home?"

"We're going to take you to the hospital first, make sure you weren't injured worse than we think. They may need to do a rape kit, and they'll take a blood test. Then you can go home."

A nearby officer volunteered to give Jordan a lift to the hospital. She was feeling battered and bruised and couldn't wait to get home and into a hot bath, but knew she would have to wait.

Chapter Twenty-seven

680 North Lake Shore Drive
November 9
10:46 A.M.

Janna had an appointment with Dr. Von Patton's psychiatrist, Dr. Lorna Shore. She was running a few minutes behind schedule.

Dr. Von Patton told her he visited a psychiatrist regularly and that he wasn't opposed to a defense of "not guilty by reason of mental defect." He told Janna his psychiatrist could confirm his history of epileptic seizures. It was entirely possible he might have mishandled a patient during an episode.

While this information was helpful, she still had to explain the doctor's seemingly unnecessary requests that his patients submit to numerous anal examinations. But she had to start somewhere, and Dr. Shore's office was as good a place as any other.

Janna arrived at the tenth-floor office and had a seat in the unattended waiting room, as Dr. Shore had instructed her. A minute later, a slender brunette woman appeared to ask if she had an appointment.

"Yes. Janna Scott. I'm waiting for Dr. Lorna Shore."

"Oh, how do you do? I'm Dr. Shore."

"Nice to meet you. Sorry I'm here a little bit later than planned."

"Don't mention it. I blocked off half an hour for you. I thought you might have changed your mind. Come on back."

Janna followed Dr. Shore back to her office. They passed several closed doors along the way, which she assumed belonged to other doctors. Once inside Dr. Shore's office, she looked around. The room was somewhat small, just large enough for a little desk, a coffee table and a couch. There were some file cabinets and a bookshelf against the wall.

"Have a seat." Dr. Shore gestured to the couch.

"I feel like a patient here," Janna joked.

The woman didn't respond and Janna decided she better get to the point of her visit.

"As I told you on the phone, I'm here because I'm representing one of your patients, Mason Von Patton, on a rather delicate matter."

"Yes, I'm aware of his situation."

"Dr. Von Patton is considering, only considering, a mental defect defense. He told me you would be aware of his medical history."

"I'm his doctor, if that's what you want to know."

"Yes, I realize that much. Would you be able to provide the court with any information or an opinion as to his mental health?"

"I'm afraid if that's what you're looking for, you've wasted your time coming down here. Everything between my patient and me is privileged information, and without a signed release from my patient I really can't share anything with you."

"Didn't Von Patton sign one for me? I told him I would be contacting you and we discussed his signing a release."

"Well he didn't sign one, so like I said, it's privileged information."

"I know all about privileges, believe me," Janna replied, undaunted by Dr. Shore. "But those privileges go out the window if you think a client is going to hurt himself or another person, correct?"

"I'm familiar with the laws, as well as the ethics of psychiatry, thank you very much, Ms. Scott. Are you suggesting I think Dr. Von Patton is going to hurt someone?"

"I'm not saying that. All I'm asking is whether you would be able to provide the court with an opinion as to Dr. Von Patton's mental health, preferably an opinion that would work in his favor?"

"I could provide the court with an opinion. Favorable or not, I don't know what you mean by that."

Janna turned the table on the doctor. "Are you trying to tell me something now? Do you think he intentionally acted against these patients?"

Dr. Shore squirmed nervously in her chair. "I've told you, anything I know is privileged at this point."

"What exactly are you suggesting?" What did this woman know about her client? Janna had seen enough elusive witnesses in her time to know Dr. Shore was hiding something.

"I'm not suggesting anything at all," the psychiatrist finally responded.

Janna wasn't convinced by her response. "You're obviously aware of his seizures. Is it possible Dr. Von Patton could have harmed a patient during a seizure? Could a seizure cause a violent episode or cause him to do something out of character?"

"I suppose it's possible."

Dr. Shore wasn't giving away information today, that much was for sure.

"Let me explain the attorney-client privilege to you," Janna offered. "I can't do anything against my client's best interest. Nothing. So whatever you tell me is safe. My privilege is far more stringent than yours. Even if Dr. Von Patton were to tell me that he was guilty of harming someone, I cannot turn him in. My job is to represent his interests, his liberties. And it is he who asked me to talk to you. I'm just here to find out if you would be willing to testify on his behalf."

Janna let this information sink in with Dr. Shore for a minute.

The doctor seemed to think it over. After a brief moment of silence, she requested that Janna ask her client to sign a medical release form.

"I don't know if I am the proper person to testify on Dr. Von Patton's behalf. If you want his records, they need to be authorized for release by the patient or subpoenaed by the courts. And even if subpoenaed, they may still be privileged. I told the man who was here the other day the same thing."

"What man?" Janna asked. She didn't have anyone working for her. Who would be here looking for Von Patton's records?

"The investigator who was here. I believe he said he was with the county."

"The county's investigator? The State's Attorney sent an investigator over here?"

"Apparently so."

"How would they even know about you?"

Janna's mind raced for an answer. The ASA assigned to this case had to request that an investigator be sent over to talk to a prospective witness, defense or prosecution. How would the ASA know to request an interview with Dr. Shore?

"The property invoice," Janna almost shouted as the answer popped into her head.

"I beg your pardon?"

160

"Dr. Von Patton's prescriptions. He was carrying them when he was arrested. They would have been noted on his property invoice. The ASA must have tracked them back to you somehow. Smart attorney."

"Why would they do that?"

"They must be anticipating an insanity or mental defect defense," Janna theorized.

"Why would they want to talk to me then? I'm his doctor."

"Exactly. Dr. Von Patton can still be found guilty even if he's suffering from a mental defect, if the State can prove that this defect would not affect him knowing right from wrong. They need to know what he's suffering from before they can prepare their own expert witness."

"I see. So you think the State's Attorney's office is checking up on him?"

"It appears that way." She sighed and started putting her coat on. "What did you tell the investigator? Can you tell me that much?"

"As I've already said. Nothing. I told him absolutely nothing. I can't even verify that Mason Von Patton is a patient of mine. Now, I've said more than enough to you. You should leave."

"I'm on my way out." She hitched her bag up onto her shoulder, brushing a loose strand of hair from her face. "Thank you for your time, Dr. Shore. I'll be requesting that my client sign a medical release."

"I'm sure you will. Have a good day, Miss Scott."

Chapter Twenty-eight

Cook County Hospital
November 9
11:12 A.M.

Dr. Von Patton was visiting his patients at the hospital, making his rounds, when he bumped into Essie.

"Good morning, nurse."

"Uh, morning, doctor."

Essie seemed nervous. She was acting strangely and stiffened up as soon as she saw him.

"What's wrong, Essie?"

"Nothing. It's just . . . well, never mind. I don't want to interrupt your rounds. It can wait."

Dr. Von Patton sensed that he wasn't going to like whatever Essie had to tell him. She was treating him differently. She was not as friendly as usual, and her eyes told him something was wrong.

"You're not interrupting my rounds. I was just finishing. Why don't you tell me what's going on? Let's go into the lounge."

Dr. Von Patton went down the hallway and pushed open the door to the staff lounge, which luckily was empty.

Essie asked if they could sit down.

"What's the problem?"

"I don't know how to say this, so I'm just going to flat out say it. An attorney called me the other day, asking questions about your work habits. She said she worked for you."

Dr. Von Patton rolled his eyes and snorted. He leaned back in the small plastic lounge chair and crossed his legs.

"Oh boy. I'm sorry. I should have warned you. I gave her your name. She wanted to know some people, staff members other than doctors, who would know my character at work, something like that."

"Oh," Essie seemed a bit surprised, but relieved at the same time. "So you do know this woman?"

"Yes, of course. She's my attorney. It just slipped my mind. I failed to mention it to you. I hope you don't mind. It's just you are generally the nurse on duty when I make my rounds. I thought you would be a good person. . . ."

"No, no. I don't mind at all," Essie said. "She just

caught me off guard, that's all. This woman calls up, says she's an attorney, and starts asking me questions about you. I wasn't sure. And I don't need any legal trouble, that's for sure."

"She's a very direct woman. I had no idea she would be calling you so soon. My apologies again."

"I didn't say much, you know. I wanted to check with you first. I told her you were a good doc, one of the best, and that I liked working with you."

"I appreciate the kind words."

"Anytime." Essie nodded, satisfied. "One more thing. Do you mind if I ask what's going on? Are you in trouble? Some kind of malpractice thing?"

Dr. Von Patton felt his cheeks flush and his face grow hot. "It's nothing, just an old malpractice claim. Nothing serious."

"Won't the hospital take care of your legal stuff on that? I thought the hospital covered all of us on those kind of claims."

"It's something from a long time ago. The hospital wasn't involved. They have no idea. And I'd rather keep if that way for now, if you can understand."

"Oh sure. I don't blame you one bit." She waved her hands in the air. "Say no more."

"Thanks. I owe you one." The doctor stood up to leave and Essie followed his cue.

"Okay. Well, I'm glad I checked with you."

"Me too."

He watched Essie leave the lounge and return to the floor. Then he sat back down at the lunch table.

What was his new attorney thinking? Calling his co-workers? Was this woman out of her mind?

He'd be without a medical license for sure if she started talking to his nurses. Janna had asked him for the names of some doctors and nurses he worked with, but he didn't realize the crazy broad was going to start calling people and harassing them for information. He needed to talk to her right away, before she took this any further.

Damn it all.

He banged his fist on the table, angry at his bad luck. This thing had gotten out of control. It was time to reel it in.

Book IV

The Whole Truth

Chapter Twenty-nine

Detective Sam Reilly had been assigned to the kidnapping of Jordan Nash. Area Two was handling the matter, since that was where Jordan Nash had come in, and also where she had gotten away from the perpetrator. Detective Reilly started looking at her file. Looked like another stinker, the kind of case that sat around so long it started to smell up the office.

The young woman had obviously been drugged. She hadn't been able to remember anything. She had been taken to the hospital, but the rape kit showed she hadn't been violated sexually. However, her blood showed positive for the presence of Rohypnol in her system.

Jordan Nash had been given "rope," "roofies," "Mexican Valium," call it what you will. Which meant she wasn't going to remember anything. The drug was ten times stronger than Valium, often making the victim forget anything that happened over the previous eight hours or even longer.

Detective Reilly had hit a dead end and he hadn't even started working the case. He pulled the victim's signed statement out and read it through for the sixth time. The victim was a crime journalist for the *Tribune*. She visited the Ram's Head Tavern regularly after work. She met the perp there and that was where he grabbed her. She remembered the man seemed familiar to her and thought he told her he was a homicide detective, which could be true or not. You couldn't trust anything out of a sex offender's mouth. The next thing she remembered was crawling out of the car, a Chevy Caprice, but she wasn't sure of the year or the color, maybe metallic blue or silver.

That was about all Jordan remembered. The guy must have slipped the roofie in her drink while they were still in the bar. Once the drug kicked in, that was it, Jordan's memory was on pause.

Detective Reilly figured he should start with the Ram's Head, find out if anyone there remembered seeing her. The bartender might remember her. She was an attractive girl, and she said she was a regular. Perhaps the bartender even saw her leave with the guy.

He would have left the case file on the bottom of his pile for the day, but the Review Unit had the results on the rope that had been wrapped around Jordan's throat when she was brought in: It had been tied in a Celtic knot, the same type of knot that had been tied around the throats of the Pilsen victims. The chief felt certain the same guy who killed the Pilsen women had moved on to the bar scene downtown. Reilly was supposed to check it out.

He had to be careful. If, like Jordan said, this guy really was one of theirs, another copper . . . who knew what he would do to avoid being caught?

But he also could have been lying to Jordan, trying to find something in common with her, something to talk to her about. As far as Reilly was concerned, he could be anyone. Probably worked at her local gas station. Who was he kidding? He had nothing at this point.

The kidnapper did leave one thing behind. Some fibers had been found on the girl's shirt. They had been sent to the crime lab for analysis. At least it was something. But with no suspect and no control sample, the results wouldn't mean much for now.

He bit his lower lip, thinking. His best starting point was the Ram's Head bartender. Someone had to have noticed this guy. He grabbed his leather coat and decided to head over to the bar to check the place over and find out who had been working that shift.

Chapter Thirty

The FORBES Center
November 9
11:27 A.M.

Dr. Von Patton was outraged when he dialed Janna Scott's office. What was this crazy woman doing to him? What was she thinking, calling his staff? Maybe his friend had been wrong about her. She didn't seem so bright after all.

He let the phone ring several times and when Janna didn't answer, he redialed her number. After about fifteen minutes of his repeated efforts, she finally answered.

"This is Janna Scott."

"It's Mason Von Patton," he said in a controlled voice.

"What can I do for you?"

"A few things. For one, you could start by not calling my fellow workers to question them about my so-called work habits."

Janna was taken aback. "We talked about this the other day. Don't you remember? I spoke to you about possibly presenting character evidence on your behalf. We decided we might be able to use some of your co-workers—nurses, doctors, maybe even a patient."

"We discussed the possibility, counselor. I do not recall giving you my consent to start calling people," the doctor said.

"Well, that's how it's done. I cannot work up a case file and prepare for a trial unless I know what the witnesses are going to say. Did you want me to just call them to the stand blindly?" Janna's tone dripped with condescension and sarcasm.

"I didn't realize we were at the trial stage. I'm sorry, when did you say the trial was? Has the jury been selected already?"

"You did request a trial, did you not?" Janna grew defensive. She was perturbed with him. "How is it you expect me to do my job, Dr. Von Patton? Did you want me to rest my case immediately after the State has finished putting on theirs? Would you like me to try and guess what these people think about you? That would require the least disruption to your life in the near future. Although I'm not certain you would like the outcome."

"How is it I am supposed to keep working and living

my life if everyone in this hospital thinks I'm some sort of criminal?"

"First of all, I did not discuss the charges or details of your case with anyone. I placed a preliminary phone call to interview a potential character witness. That's it. I asked her a few basic questions, for my own purposes, to determine if I could use her or not."

"I have a reputation to think of, Miss Scott. Unlike yourself, I've spent years building a respectable practice and name in my work community. I'd like to keep it that way."

"If you don't think I am competent to handle your case, you're welcome to select another attorney."

"I think you'll do just fine. I chose you because you're a woman. Don't think I haven't thought this through." Dr. Von Patton enjoyed revealing to Janna his main criterion in selecting her. Let her know what he thought of her.

"Not well enough, obviously," Janna mumbled on the other end, ignoring his dig at her gender. "You're going to have a lot more to worry about than your reputation in the medical community if you're found guilty at this trial. I don't think I need to tell you your medical license is on the line here."

"No, you needn't remind me of that fact. By the time this trial takes place, I'm not going to have a practice left, not at this rate anyway. So I won't have much need for my license, will I?"

"You can look at it however you wish. The fact remains that I need to build a case file. We have to present our side to the court. Which right now primarily consists of character evidence and the lack of physical evidence from the victims. If things go well, we won't have to put you on the stand. We discussed this already."

"I thought we discussed a mental defect defense, temporary loss of control due to my seizures. And you mentioned something about the patients consenting to the exams."

"I'm not sure the consent defense is going to work. I'm researching that issue. Regardless, we still need the character evidence to show that your actions on the days in question must have been the result of a mental defect, as they were so out of character. Either it didn't happen at all, or if it did, it happened during a seizure. Do you understand?"

The doctor sighed. What choice did he have? He either was going to have to prepare this case for trial or take a plea, which wasn't happening.

"This whole thing is completely outrageous! It's all ridiculous! These women are lying. Can't you prove that somehow? You're leaving me with barely any room to breathe here!" Dr. Von Patton yelled.

"I don't need to remind you that there are two victims here, which makes it a little difficult to challenge credibility. Maybe with one, but not two. One woman might be lying, but it's not as easy to believe that both are. Given the fact that these two women don't know one another it would be pretty tough to get a jury to buy a conspiracy theory. And for what? Why would these women do that? That's the way the jury is going to see it. We have to give them something else."

"So that's it? Just move on to mental defect then?"

"I'm offering you the chance to get out of this thing, to walk away clean. But it's not going to be easy. It'll take some effort and in the event of a trial there may be some humiliation. Your other choice is to plead out."

"Not a chance. I'll lose my license for sure." He paused. "Miss Scott, allow me to enlighten you with my belief about our so-called justice system. As I see it, the law is nothing more than a historical interpretation of fact, twisted as needed to fit into the public opinion of the time. Look at the Dred Scott case. Lawyers are a joke. So, let me give you a history lesson—"

"No, let me give you a history lesson," Janna interrupted. "Let's start with Napoleon Bonaparte all the way up through Bill Gates. The lesson is don't let your arrogance get the better of you. Arrogance brings down countries, companies, and it can bring down even you, doctor. Don't think you're going to beat the system, or you'll lose. The key is to work within it. And that's what my role is here, to guide you through this system with as few scars as possible. Now, you will listen to me as your attorney, or I will not handle this case. You got it?"

Dr. Von Patton was stunned by her sudden outburst. She had remained calm throughout most of the phone call, but apparently had lost her patience with him.

"Are we clear?" Janna asked.

"Perfectly," he said through tight lips. "Very inspiring speech, counselor," he mumbled.

"I'll call you in a few days. And by the way, if you want me to pursue a mental defect defense, I'm going to need the medical records from your psychiatrist and whomever else you've seen for the seizures."

"I'll get right on that," he said snidely.

"Thank you." Janna hung up.

Dr. Von Patton placed the receiver back gently on its cradle, pondering his next move. He didn't trust this woman. Perhaps it hadn't been such a good idea to insult her or to lose control, but she had pushed him with her stupid ideas and comments.

He left his office and went in to see his next patient, but within a few minutes, he felt a sharp pain shoot across the back of his head. He winced and excused himself from the examination room.

He went to the bathroom and splashed some cold water on his face, trying to calm himself. His hands were shaking as he swallowed two Xanax tablets and a Tegretol, waiting for their effects to wash over him. He leaned against the cool bathroom tile, welcoming the icy feeling against his back.

He couldn't work under these conditions much longer.

Chapter Thirty-one

Beaubien Woods
South Chicago
November 9
2:54 P.M.

Susie and Steve came around the edge of the trees and found themselves on the riverbank.

"This whole thing is silly," Susie, a young blonde, complained. "Why are we out here? Whose dumb idea was it to tape this episode?"

"It was Bullman's. You think I wanted to come out here? The dude's a nut."

"We've pretty much scoped out the whole area. He can come back in here tomorrow night with his camera crew. I'm not having anything else to do with it."

Susie emphatically crossed her arms and refused to walk any farther. "Let's go back to the car, Steve."

"I agree. There's nothing else we can do in here."

Susie Benson and Steve Magna worked for a local radio broadcaster who had recently started his own television program, consisting of broadcast segments and live stunts. He was always looking for a new thrill. The latest involved a midnight escapade into the supposedly cult-filled Beaubien Woods, to try to spy on the cult members. It was going to be a real-life version of *The Blair Witch Project*. Susie and Steve, two production assistants, had been assigned the task of going into the woods during daylight to provide Bullman with a general map of the area. Bullman was daring, but not that daring. He wanted to know exactly how to get out of there if trouble started.

Steve suggested they walk down by the river and cut back through the woods until they reached the front of the preserve.

"Fine," Susie pouted, unhappy with the assignment on the whole and dreading the walk back to the car. She followed Steve along the river's edge for several minutes, but then suddenly stopped, just a few yards ahead.

"Oh my God, Steve," she stammered.

"What?" he replied, agitated with his cohort.

"L-look, over there." Susie pointed to the river's edge.

"It's a garbage bag."

"Look closer. There's an arm floating out of the bag in the water."

"Oh my . . . you're right, Suz," Steve whispered. Sure enough, there was a large trash bag lying on the river's edge, water lapping up into the bag. And from the top of the bag, a woman's arm dangled into the river.

"Holy crap! What do we do?" Steve asked.

"We have to call the police."

"Do you have your cell phone?"

"Yes. But let's get out of here first."

"Don't you think we should wait for them here? I mean how are we going to direct them back here?"

"You're the one who made the map."

"I know. But I still think we should wait here for them."

Susie didn't look so certain.

"Just give me the phone," Steve demanded.

He called 911.

"They'll be here soon," he promised Susie after hanging up.

It didn't take long for the officers to show up and secure the crime scene. They wanted to know if Steve or Susie had touched or moved anything.

"Are you kidding? I'm not going near that body," Susie said.

"Me neither. We've been sitting up on this ridge all along. Susie wasn't going to stay past dusk. It's a good thing you guys got here when you did, or she would have had my butt back at the car."

The responding officers questioned the two briefly

and told them they could leave as soon as the Area Two detectives arrived. Shortly after, both the area detectives and the medical examiner showed up. They talked to Susie and Steve, then asked one of the R.O.s to walk them to their car.

The woman's corpse was pulled from the river's edge and out of the trash bag. She had been dead for a couple of days. The first thing the medical examiner noticed, as did anyone standing near the body, was the large cross that had been carved into the dead woman's stomach. She also had a noose fastened around her neck.

"It's our boy from over in Pilsen," Detective Bronson announced. All the Chicago area detectives had been made aware of the emerging serial killer.

"You bet it is."

"Let's pull her out and get her to the morgue for autopsy," the medical examiner instructed.

"It's going to be a long night." Detective Bronson shook his head, wishing the sick freak hadn't come down to Area Two. "We better get word over to Area Four. How many is this anyway?"

"I think it's number four," Detective Glover, another Area Two detective, said.

The evidence technician was trying to collect what little he could from the woman's remains.

"I don't know how much we're going to be able to get off her. This guy threw her almost into the river. The one hand is dry, though, and it looks like she's got something under her thumbnail." The technician wrapped the woman's hand with a plastic bag and taped it closed around her wrist, preserving any evidence under her fingernails.

The technician held up the vial. "Looks like a piece of tape or something. I'm going to try and pull some fibers from under the rest of her fingernails," he said.

Detective Glover walked away from the body and up onto a small ridge where Bronson was already standing. "I don't think the department is going to be able to keep this out of the press much longer. They're not going to be able to deny it's a serial killer."

"Nope. And it looks like the reporters are here already," Detective Bronson said, looking away from the body and up toward the street. On the I-94 bridge that crossed over the Calumet River and Beaubien Woods, a camera crew was setting up.

"Damn it. They must have picked it up on the scanner," Bronson said, glancing back down at the body.

"The word is out," Glover chimed in.

"All right. I better get a report filed for the chief. Let him sort this mess out. With bodies popping up all over the city, we're bound to have a few cooks in the kitchen, if you know what I mean."

"I'll catch up with you later," Detective Glover told him.

"Sure thing."

Bronson told one of the younger officers to deal with the reporters before anyone else did.

"Tell them they have to contact the department for an official statement!" he yelled after the officer.

"I know, don't worry," the officer called back.

"Damn it all to hell. Why couldn't you keep yourself in Area Four?" he said out loud to the woods.

Chapter Thirty-two

Detective Stone heard about Jordan Nash and also that another body had been discovered yesterday afternoon in Beaubien Woods. Apparently the killer had moved on from the local prostitutes. Stone heard Area Two was handling both cases, but he was to work with them as needed.

The Beaubien Woods victim was a hair stylist who had been missing for several days. Stone planned to get the report first thing that morning. However, when he arrived at the station, the forensics and autopsy reports on the third victim, the last woman found in Pilsen, were waiting for him on his desk.

Stone looked at the forensics report first. Blue polyester and gray wool fiber strands were found underneath the woman's fingernails. As of yet, the police had not been able to give the lab a control sample for the fiber strands. They still didn't have a suspect and nothing to compare the samples to, other than the fibers found on the other dead women.

The crime lab results confirmed that the fiber strands from all three victims matched, at least the blue strands. The gray fibers were a new addition. The fiber analysis said the gray strands were 100% wool, dyed medium gray. It didn't help much, but Stone knew he was lucky to have gotten anything at all from forensics on the fiber strands. The victim had been dumped in water, so any trace evidence that might have been left behind was destroyed, except the fibers taken from under the woman's fingernails.

The autopsy report on the third victim was just what Stone expected. She had been strangled, found with a rope tied around her neck, fastened in a Celtic knot. A cross had been carved into her hand. No surprises there. And like the previous victims, this woman had bite marks on her breasts and inner thighs. Photos had been sent to the forensic odontologist.

Stone sighed. He had been half asleep last night when he heard on the news that the most recent victim, the hair stylist, had a cross carved into her stomach. The reporters were all over this thing now, which meant the heat was going to come down on him. He was upset he hadn't been called. Damn Area

Two, probably trying to keep it on their own turf. They wanted their own guys working the case, most likely.

What really bothered him was that the killer was clearly getting more aggressive, more violent, not only with his victim choice, but in leaving his mark behind.

Stone looked up from the reports when Arnie strode into the office. His skin was sallow and he seemed more tired than usual.

"Hey pardner, whassup?" Stone said.

"Not much," Arnie replied flatly, plopping himself down into a chair.

"Not in the mood for my reindeer games today?"

"Nah," Arnie muttered unenthusiastically.

"We've got reports back on victim number three." Stone held up the files. "And I suppose you heard they found another body in Beaubien Woods last night? The press has really sunk their teeth into this thing. The chief's gonna be on us."

"On you, maybe. Not me."

"What do you mean? You got some kind of departmental immunity I don't know about?"

"Hardly," Arnie answered, fidgeting with his hands. "I have to tell you something, Stone."

"Shoot. What do you got?"

"What I got is IA on my ass."

"What? What are you talking about, Arnie? You're not making sense."

Stone was genuinely concerned for his partner. Normally upbeat, Arnie had been sullen and with-

186

drawn lately. And Stone couldn't seem to get anything out of him.

"Internal Affairs. They called me in yesterday afternoon."

"Oh yeah? That's where you were, huh?"

"I didn't want to say anything to you. Not at first. I thought it was just some routine crap, you know."

Stone didn't know, but he didn't want to say anything that might upset his partner further.

"Sure. What did they want?" he asked.

Arnie took a long, deep breath. "It seems I'm being accused of . . . I don't even know how to tell you this."

"Just say it. Whatever it is, you know you've got me behind you."

"I'm being accused of conduct unbefitting an officer or some crap like that. A couple of call girls, I mean we're talking hookers here, Jack, dumb hookers. They're saying I took sexual favors from them in exchange for lowering or dropping their charges. Or not arresting them at all. IA has a report with a charge of prostitution that was crossed out and changed to indecent exposure or something. I don't even know what it says."

"What? That's all they got? That's ridiculous. They're gonna take the word of some hooker over you? Come on. I've been with you out on the streets. I've never seen anything like that. I'll be happy to tell them that, too."

Arnie's voice was barely a whisper. "It happened when we went in on a raid over at that apartment

187

building on Wells. Remember that escort service we busted a few months ago?"

"Yeah, I do."

"A couple of women said while I was in there, you know, I made them go down on me, that kind of thing."

"Did you, Arnie?" Stone asked softly.

"I don't know what I did. I don't even know anymore." Arnie's chest heaved and Stone thought he was going to start sobbing.

"Hey, Arnie, they'll straighten this thing out. You know they will. And you can count on my support." Stone put his arm around the shoulders of his long-time partner and friend.

"What can I do for you?"

"There is one thing. And I hate to even ask you to do it," Arnie said.

"What is it?" Stone hoped his partner wasn't about to ask him what he thought.

Chapter Thirty-three

1918 South Indiana
November 10
5:43 A.M.

Dr. Von Patton couldn't sleep. He got up to pee for the second time that hour. His eyes were heavy and his body craved rest, yet he had lain awake in his bed staring at the ceiling for hours.

He rinsed his mouth with Listerine and washed his face. He decided to go to the hospital early. Understandably, he had been having difficulty concentrating on his patients and his research lately. Maybe an early start would help.

After pouring himself a large glass of orange juice, he guzzled it down with a Xanax and left for the hospital. He dressed quickly and went out to his Mercedes.

He decided to ride through the neighborhoods that morning and turned down Cermak to head over to Ashland. Within several minutes he was driving through the Pilsen neighborhood.

As he drove down Ashland Avenue, he noticed the small row houses as he passed. They all looked the same to him. He passed several rows of empty, abandoned buildings. They seemed familiar. Maybe it was just that they were so similar. Or maybe he had seen them on the news. Wasn't this where that woman's body had been found?

As he passed by a broken-down, forgotten two flat on the corner of Ashland and 19th Street a painful bolt shot across the back of his neck. His concentration fluttered, and he felt as if he was having déjà vu. Images started to flash before his eyes, and he was forced to pull the car to the side of the road.

What was wrong with him? It wasn't a seizure. It was something else.

It had to be the side effects from the Tegretol that were bothering him. Sweat beads formed on his brow and began to drip down his face. His hands were twitching and he felt ill. It might simply be that he was exhausted. Another image flashed in front of his eyes, of a woman's face.

Who was it? He didn't recognize her. Then he saw her again. The woman looked like Essie. What was happening to him?

Dr. Von Patton was scared. He didn't know what his

own body was doing, and he didn't like it. He made the rest of the trip quickly and hurried into the hospital.

Why had that abandoned building bothered him so much? And why Essie Ruiz's face flashing before him?

The doctor was confused and worried. Something terrible was wrong with him. His head was pounding and he felt completely worn out. He needed to lie down. But first he went to the hospital chapel.

He strolled into the small chapel and walked right up to the altar area. A cross hung from the wall behind the altar. He got down on his knees and prayed. He prayed for the seizures to stop, for his court case to pass quickly and for his research to be completed. He knew he couldn't take much more of this stress or that wicked creature, Kelsey Dore. It had to stop sometime.

Why was this happening to him? What had he done to deserve it?

After a few minutes he left the chapel and went to lie down in his office. Unable to sleep, he closed his eyes and tried to stop his mind from racing, thinking of all the horrible possibilities that might lie ahead. What was he going to do?

Chapter Thirty-four

Janna inhaled deeply, letting the cool apple-flavored smoke fill her lungs, before blowing a stream of it at the yellow canoe-shaped light fixture hanging from the steeple ceiling. She leaned back into the tangerine and purple cushions against the wall and giggled.

"I can't believe I'm doing this."

"It's fun, isn't it?" Detective Jack Stone asked.

"A blast. Are you sure this is legal?" she teased.

"Do you see me arresting anyone?"

"It just looks so much like a bong. I haven't seen anything like this since college."

Janna had already drunk three Heinekens and felt

192

pretty good. The two were having dinner at Tork, a Middle Eastern restaurant. Stone wanted to take her someplace original for their first date. He had certainly succeeded.

The two dined on *muhammara* and *samak kosheri* for appetizers and Janna had ordered lamb kebabs for her entrée. The food was sumptuous, and the romantic atmosphere added to the energy between her and Jack Stone.

Small crannies filled with votive candles speckled the plaster walls, casting an amber glow across the room. A Middle Eastern band played, setting the perfect ambiance for the belly dancer who was making her way around the floor, clanging her thumb cymbals high above her head.

Stone ordered a *hookah* pipe for them, a tall glass water pipe filled with apple tobacco. The hookah had been brought to the table and they were both enjoying the experience. Janna took the wooden handle and drew in deeply off the disposable plastic tip.

It was her first official date with Stone, and actually, her first date in several months. She had been so occupied with her new office she hadn't spent much time searching for companionship.

Stone caught her off guard when he asked her out, but to her pleasant surprise, she was really enjoying herself. She had known him for several years, but had never taken their relationship outside of work. The *hookah* and the Heinekens had loosened her up and she felt relaxed sitting against the large fluffy pillows.

"So you're really representing the other half these days?" Stone asked.

"I sure am," Janna replied.

"You gonna be pulling up in your BMW soon, like all the other defense attorneys?"

"I don't think so," she snorted. "Not unless they're giving them away."

"Why'd you switch over anyway?"

"I don't know. The office politics got so bad. And truthfully, I got sick of sending these young kids to jail, you know? I mean half of them were only twenty years old or so. Just kids with no opportunities, no role models. Most of them aren't any kind of real criminals. Drug addicts, rookie dealers . . . you know how it is."

"I do. But there are a few really rotten ones that make you feel pretty good about what you're doing. And then there are the victims."

"I know. But that wasn't enough anymore."

"So you're paying your penance by defending them now?"

"No. It's my background, though. The way I look at it, my job is only to make sure that the State does theirs. To make sure the State proves their case beyond a reasonable doubt. Someone has to keep them honest."

"That what you tell yourself?"

"You can't stop giving me grief about this, can you? To be honest, I am somewhat ambivalent about the defense side. Especially with my current client list."

"Oh yeah? What kind of stuff are you handling?"

"A couple drug cases. One sexual assault."

"Rape case?"

"No, a doctor actually. He's accused of molesting patients. The sad thing is, that's one of my better clients."

"Sounds like a real charmer. That the guy you were asking about the other day? The one who was brought into Central?"

"The very same," Janna said slowly, reaching for the *hookah* pipe again.

"You're really enjoying that thing, huh?"

"I am," she admitted.

"I'm enjoying watching you smoke it." He laughed at her as she took a huge drag from the tube.

"So what about you? How long have you been a detective?"

"Over fifteen years."

"You still happy with it?"

"I guess. A lot's been going on lately. This serial killer has gotten pretty scary. The department's still trying to keep it low profile, but the guy is definitely out of control. And, talk about bad timing, my partner just got suspended."

"Oh no. How come?"

"Ah, I don't really want to get into the whole thing. He's been suspended temporarily for misconduct or something, so they say."

"I'm sorry to hear that." She could tell Stone was bothered by the subject and changed the conversation topic.

"What about this killer? Do you have any leads, any suspects?"

"Not at the moment. We're working on it, though. Four dead women so far. And one victim who escaped."

"You mean someone got away from the guy?"

"We think so. Happened down in Area Two. I'm not working on the kidnapping case, though. Area Two is handling it. I'm working off the Pilsen victims." Stone rubbed his temples and scanned the smoke-filled room for the waitress. "You want to order dessert?"

"Sure, if you do. Let's share."

He glanced at the menu, then ordered a banana chocolate torte for the two of them.

"Did you ever kill anyone while you were on duty?" Janna asked.

"You sure know how to make light dinner conversation on a date," Stone said with a laugh.

"I know, I know. I'm sorry. I haven't been on a date in a while," she admitted. "I guess I'm out of practice."

Stone was staring at her intensely. His eyes seemed dark and mysterious in the light. There was a strange energy around him. He was looking at her kind of oddly, she thought. Maybe it was the *hookah*, she decided.

"The answer is no. Never have. Shot a couple people, but never killed anyone," Stone finally said. "How about you?"

"What do you mean?" She was puzzled.

"How many people have you sent to the chair?"

Janna looked stunned.

"Two can play at this game, counselor."

"Now who's making the light dinner conversation!" It was her turn to poke fun at him. "I think I need another hit off that pipe before I can answer that one."

"Maybe these are the questions Chuck Woolery should have asked."

"Would have made *The Dating Game* a lot more interesting, that's for sure."

"I guess."

The two were clearly enjoying each other's company and Janna didn't want the date to end.

"So really, have you ever sent anyone to the chair? Figuratively speaking, of course."

"It's a question in the interview process," Janna said.

"What is?"

"How you feel about the death penalty. They ask you that."

"Really? You're kidding?"

"Absolutely not."

"That makes sense, though."

"But yes, I've tried a couple of cases that ended up in death sentences."

"Is it hard?"

"Yes. And if it wasn't, you probably shouldn't be doing it. You have to think about it, you know? I would think, what if my argument is the convincing factor, the reason the jurors come back with the death penalty? That man's blood is on my hands, in a way. It was my argument that sent him there."

"But it really isn't. It's what the guy did."

"That's what I would tell myself, but it's hard after a

while. This person's life hangs in the balance and you're arguing for his death. And the only guidelines to help the jurors decide is some statute written by a bunch of legislators in Springfield. It's troubling."

"Then I guess there's only one thing left to say."

"What's that?"

"Here's to the defendants." Stone lifted his beer glass, offering a toast.

"To the defendants." Janna clanked her glass against his and finished her beer. She was feeling light-headed and out of it. She stood up to find the ladies' room. "I'll be back in two and two," she joked.

"I'll be waiting." Stone laughed loudly, almost eerily.

A chill ran down her spine as she walked away.

Chapter Thirty-five

680 North Lake Shore Drive
Chicago, Illinois
November 13
11:38 A.M.

Jordan couldn't help wondering whether she had made the right decision in coming to Dr. Underwood. She'd heard about him through word-of-mouth and he came highly recommended, but that didn't ease her nerves any. Not much did as of late.

She hadn't slept in days for fear of her nightmares. When she tried to sleep, she would wake up in a cold sweat. She had been staying with her mother for the past several days and hadn't left the house until today. She had severe panic attacks sporadically throughout each day and into the night. Now, she couldn't even bear to turn off the lights to sleep, and the dark circles around her eyes showed it. Jordan was frazzled and knew she couldn't continue on in this state.

Her brother-in-law mentioned a woman from his work who, after being attacked in a parking lot, had a difficult time returning to the office. The woman had found Dr. Underwood, a forensic psychotherapist, and claimed he had helped her immensely. Jordan had taken the recommendation and was about to find out for herself.

Dr. Underwood was a healing doctor, using hypnosis only to help his patients reach a state of relaxation and find the inner peace they knew prior to the traumatic event. Jordan had been sitting on his sofa for the past several minutes listening to his explanation of the hypnosis process as he attempted to dispel her misconceptions and the myths surrounding its use.

"So what are you saying? That you have no control over me while I'm hypnotized?" Jordan didn't believe him.

"It's true. It's a self-imposed state. You need to understand that. Basically, I guide you into a complete and total state of relaxation. But it's you who allows it to happen. You are always in control, Jordan, remember that."

"And I can have my mom in here with me?"

"Absolutely. The therapy path is entirely up to you. You chart your own course." Dr. Underwood smiled, hoping to instill confidence in her with his soft voice and his gentle manner. She stared at him, unconvinced. This guy was crazier than she was, she thought.

"I think I want my mom here. At least for the first time."

"Okay. Let's bring her in then."

Jordan stood up to get her mother from the waiting room. When she returned, Dr. Underwood had pulled his chair closer to the armchair where Jordan would sit for the hypnosis.

"Mom, you sit over there." She directed her mother to the couch.

"Hello, doctor," Susan Nash said. "I'm a little nervous. You'll have to forgive me."

"Me too, Mom." Jordan cracked a sliver of a smile.

"As I was discussing with your daughter, the point of this exercise is entirely for healing purposes. She tells me she cannot remember her abduction or anything surrounding the event, yet she is gripped, almost paralyzed, with fear at the very thought of leaving the house, going to sleep, even turning out the lights.

"Our only goal here is to help Jordan retrieve enough memory to successfully overcome the trauma distortion factor. You see, Mrs. Nash, the conscious mind desires to repress unpleasant memories. We all do this on a daily basis. In the case of severe trauma, memories are sometimes lost through a basic shorting out of the nerve synapses. The rational part of the brain simply shuts down and our survival instinct takes over. It is very common in trauma victims."

201

"I see. And what if Jordan can't handle what she remembers?"

"Again, we're only trying to have enough memory surface so that Jordan can feel in control of the situation. We can do post-traumatic counseling to deal with additional feelings triggered by the process."

"Additional feelings? Is this going to make it worse?" Jordan asked.

"No, I promise that much. You may feel scared as some of these feelings emerge, but the plan is to help you get through the feelings, in a controlled fashion, and to help direct you to the healing phase. This process will allow you to remember and overcome the traumatic event."

"How long will this take, doctor?" Mrs. Nash asked.

"About an hour. Depending on how it goes today, we'll probably only need to do one or two hypnosis sessions. Afterward, Jordan will need to come for a few regular counseling sessions."

"Will I remember specific things about the attack after this?"

"Some memories may come back to you after we open the door today, but I will give you the tools and the suggestions to deal with those memories that do surface. We are only trying to recover enough to get you over the hump."

"Should I tell the police what I remember?"

"As we discussed, the police and the courts do not allow any type of testimony or evidence that is linked to or comes from hypnosis. If I hypnotize you, you will not be able to testify against your attacker. You do understand this, don't you?"

"I don't care. I just want to get better. I can't remember anything on my own, and I feel worse with each passing day. The police said it would be very difficult for me to testify anyway, since the blood results show I was drugged. They said the attorneys would tear my testimony apart. They don't want me as a witness."

"Okay. Let's get started then."

Jordan's hands gripped the armrests, her fingernails digging into the cushiony fabric.

"All right. Here we go."

Dr. Underwood dimmed the lights and drew the shades in the office. His slow, monotone voice guided Jordan down in minutes. He asked her a few questions to make sure she was thoroughly relaxed and in a calm place but still functioning effectively. Then he prepared to lead her to the day of the attack.

"Okay, Jordan. Now you are going to review a special documentary film of a sequence of events. The film can be stopped, reversed, fast-forwarded, freeze-framed, or played in slow motion to provide you with an opportunity to review any segment more closely. Do you understand these instructions?"

"Yes," Jordan nodded.

"The sequence of events in the documentary may seem traumatic. You are only watching the documentary and will remain calm and relaxed. You are only reporting the events, as an investigative reporter would do. Do you understand?"

"Yes." Jordan nodded her head again.

Dr. Underwood regressed her to the day in question. "Let us go to the early, early morning of November 8th of this year. Are you there?"

"Yes."

"Where are you? Do you recognize anything?"

"I'm leaving work. The *Tribune* building on Michigan Avenue. I am walking to the Ram's Head Tavern."

"Are you on the street, the sidewalk, a bridge, a staircase?" It was important Dr. Underwood not lead Jordan into answers. Her mind needed to arrive at conclusions on its own, to fill in any blanks without his direction. For this reason, he would ask her very little about the attack. He just needed to elicit enough information during hypnosis to be able to treat her successfully.

"I'm on a staircase, a cement staircase, going down."

"Are you walking with someone or are you alone?"

"I'm alone."

"Do you see anyone else on the staircase or in front of you?"

"No. No one else is there."

"Do you know what time it is?"

"No. It is early morning, though."

"Is it light outside or is it dark?"

"Dark."

"Okay. What is happening in the documentary now?"

"Now I'm in the Ram's Head Tavern. Sal is bartending. There is a drink on the bar in front of me."

"Is it your drink?"

"I don't know."

"Are you touching the drink?"

"Yes. I'm drinking it."

"Is anyone else with you?"

"No. Just Sal."

"Look around the bar. Do you recognize anyone else?"

"There are some other reporters there. Jimmy. And Artie."

"Let's fast forward a little."

"Okay."

"Do you see anyone new in the bar?"

Jordan paused and took a deep breath before responding. "Yes."

"Do you recognize this person?"

"Yes."

"Is it a man or a woman?"

"A man."

"Do you know his name?"

"No."

"What is the man doing?"

"He's sitting next to me. He's talking to me."

"What is he saying to you?"

"He's talking to me about my work. He says he's a detective."

"Okay. Let's fast-forward again. What's happening now?"

"I don't know. I'm stumbling. The man is holding me up. We're walking toward a car."

"What does the car look like? Can you describe it?"

"It's a sedan. Like a cop car, kind of. It has four doors and it's light blue or silver."

"Okay. That's good, Jordan." He backed off a little. He didn't want to push her too hard in the first session.

"Is the man talking to you?"

"Yes. He's saying not to worry. Everything is going to be fine. He's going to take care of me. He's pushing me into the car."

"Are you resisting?"

"No. I'm too tired."

"Are you inside of the car?"

"Yes."

"Do you see anything?"

"No. I'm lying in the backseat. I'm wrapped in a wool blanket. It's itching my skin, my face."

"Can you fast-forward again?"

"Yes."

"What's happening now?"

"I've been in the car for a long time. I'm hot and itchy. The car's stopped a couple of times, I think."

"What else? What do you feel?"

"There's something around my neck." Jordan picked her hands up, holding them next to her face, around her neck.

Mrs. Nash, concerned for her daughter, inched forward on the sofa.

"Jordan, can you see what's on your neck? Can you touch it?"

"Yes. It's some kind of rope."

206

"Can you fast-forward again?"

"Yes."

"Are you still in the car?"

"Yes. The car has been driving for a while. I think we're on a highway. We're stopped again. I can see something."

"What do you see?"

"A sign."

"Okay, good. What does it say? Can you read it?"

"N-A-T, something. I can't tell, maybe National. Maybe a bank sign? I can't read it."

"That's all right. Can you see the driver?"

"No. Only the back of his head."

"Can you see what he's wearing?"

"A baseball hat. White Sox. A tan barn jacket."

"Is it the same man from the bar?"

"Yes."

"Okay, what's happening now?"

"He's getting out of the car. He isn't coming back."

"What's going on?"

"I'm sitting up. I feel sick, tired."

"Are you hurt in any way?"

"No. Just my neck."

"Has anyone else been in the car with you besides the driver?"

"No."

"Okay, let's fast-forward once more."

Dr. Underwood took Jordan through her escape from the vehicle and then led her back to full consciousness.

"When I reach ten you will be fully awake, refreshed, and relaxed." Jordan licked her lips, sitting calmly in the armchair. The doctor was counting.

"Ten," he finally said, emphatically.

Jordan's eyes slowly peeled open and adjusted to the dim lighting.

"Jordan, I'm going to ask you a few questions now."

"All right."

Dr. Underwood made sure she was dehypnotized and reorientated and then concluded their session.

"You did great," he said. "Now remember, things may come back to you later on, about that day," he warned her. "You can call me if anything troubling happens or if you are having negative thoughts or feelings."

"Okay, thank you. So what happened?"

"I think we're going to be able to pull you through this just fine," the doctor told her. "You're going to be all right."

"When should I come back?"

"Why don't you give it a couple of days. We can do one more hypnosis session and then we'll get started on some self-hypnosis and breathing exercises. Things you can do to help yourself. Sound good?"

"Sounds great."

Jordan and her mother left. She felt slightly better and was eager to return in a few days. She knew she had to be strong if she was going to get through this.

Chapter Thirty-six

Sarah looked at James, still lying motionless in his bed. She had grown kind of attached to him, maybe only because he caused her the least trouble. There was something about him that she liked, though. She was worried for him. She learned that the hospital would have to transfer him out soon. He was no longer an emergency care patient and would be transferred either to Clayton Health or the state mental hospital.

The hospital's jail section often became overcrowded and they couldn't afford to lose a bed to James if he wasn't progressing. The doctors determined James might remain in his current state, drifting in and out of consciousness, for months. There was no telling how long it may take for him to fully recover.

Sarah walked over to James and felt his forehead with the back of her hand. His head was cool. She talked to him a little. When she removed her hand from his head, his eyes snapped open, and for an instant, he seemed to recognize her.

His eyes, wide with wonder, bored holes into her chest. Weak, he grabbed her arm and tried to pull her down to his cracked lips.

"Doctor! Doctor!" he whispered loudly.

"No, the doctor isn't here. It's me, Sarah, your nurse."

Sarah didn't want to leave his bedside. This was the first intelligible thing James had said for days. Maybe he was starting to come around. Maybe this time he would stay with them.

"Don't let 'em take me," James moaned. "Don't let the boog man take me!"

"You mean the boogie man?"

"The boogie man, the doctor."

"The doctor ain't no boogie man. He's here to help you." Sarah tried to soothe James. His eyes were still wide open and he seemed frightened.

Suddenly exhausted, James fell back on his pillow.

What did he mean "Don't let them take me"? Had he heard her thoughts just now? Had he heard the doctors talking earlier? Did he know he was going to be transferred out of Cook County?

The poor man was still talking about boogie men

and demons. He made no sense. If he kept this up, they would stick him in the mental hospital for sure.

Sarah planned to talk to the doctors. Maybe they should wait a few more days. This was definitely a sign of improvement. He had been almost conversational with her. It showed hope that he might recover, and if he stayed at Cook County, it was all the more likely.

Chapter Thirty-seven

Cook County Hospital
November 13
10:26 A.M.

Essie approached the door of the small office Dr. Von Patton used when he was at the hospital. She planned to leave a patient chart he had requested on his desk. When she opened the door, the office was dark. He must not be coming in today, she thought. Usually he made his rounds at Cook County early in the morning, but she still hadn't seen him on the floor.

Essie walked into the office and over to the doctor's desk. Its mahogany-stained surface was cluttered with paper. The doctor was not usually this careless with his work. His office was the messiest she had seen it, and things seemed to be in a state of disarray.

She glanced through the papers on his desk. There were several charts from HIV patients over at Clayton Health Services, the jail's medical facility. She flipped through one of the patient's charts.

Patient showed no response to usual treatments or medications. HIV has progressed to full-blown AIDS. Deterioration rapid.

She briefly scanned the rest of the chart. She didn't know how Dr. Von Patton could work with so many diseased and suffering people. Most of them had no hope for recovery, much less survival. It had to be disheartening to have most of your patients die on you. It certainly was for her as a nurse.

She shuffled through some more papers on his desk and noticed a piece of letterhead with his lawyer's name, Janna Scott. She glanced at the letter, but did not pick it up.

She eyed the letter again. She did want to know why the doctor was in trouble. Why he had his own private attorney and wasn't using the hospital's legal staff. She thought about picking up the letter. After all, this woman was calling her, and the doctor had asked for her help. She deserved to know something. She decided to read it. He would never know.

Essie pulled the letter from beneath the pile it was buried under. Then she heard the doorknob turn. She dropped the letter on the top of the pile and looked up quickly, startled. Dr. Von Patton was standing in the doorway.

"What are you doing in here?" he asked her suspiciously.

"I was just leaving those patient charts you asked me about," she stammered, backing away from the desk.

"Where? On the bottom of the papers on my desk? I'm not likely to find them there, am I?"

"No. I just . . . I was straightening your desk, so you would see the charts. There's no room for them. I didn't want them to get lost in all this paper," she explained nervously.

"Then put them on the chair next time. Please."

"Okay. I'm sorry. I was only trying to be helpful."

"Thank you, Miss Ruiz. Now if you don't mind, I have work to do. I'm late as it is."

"Certainly. I'm getting right out of your way."

Essie scampered past the doctor and out his door, flustered by their encounter. She hadn't learned anything and now Dr. Von Patton thought she had been snooping in his office.

Pure genius, Essie.

The fact that she had actually been snooping only made her feel worse. Why couldn't she just mind her own business?

Chapter Thirty-eight

O'Hare Marriott
November 13
1:12 P.M.

The Chicago Police Department and the Cook County State's Attorney's Office rented a large conference room at the Marriott. They called anyone investigating the "Cross-Town Killer," a name the killer recently had been christened with by the papers. The prosecutors, the Chief of Detectives, the Area Four detectives, the Area Two detectives, and any officer who might be remotely involved with some aspect of the murders, all were in the room.

Detective Stone, who was still investigating the Pilsen murders, took a seat near the exit. The room was packed, and the chief asked everyone to quiet down.

"All right. We're here to try to bring this thing to some order. Within four weeks we've got four bodies and one kidnapping victim who is believed to have escaped from the killer's car. So far this guy has taken women from the North Side and the South Side. We've found bodies in Pilsen and Beaubien Woods. The kidnapping victim was taken from the central Loop area and escaped on the South Side. He's working the city. Which means some competition might spring up between the different Areas."

The chief cleared his throat and took a long look around the room filled with cops before he continued. "I'm here, with the State's Attorney's Office and the Internal Affairs Division," the chief nodded toward two men in suits standing to his right, "to remind you that we have very clear standards of conduct in this department. Any breach of those standards, of department policy, will be handled promptly and without leniency. I repeat, we will strictly enforce the rules of this department during the course of this investigation."

The murmurs from behind the bench-style tables quieted completely. The room was silent. The chief was serious about this investigation, and everyone knew it.

"I expect full cooperation with your fellow officers. All reporters or any requests from the press should be referred to the Correspondence Division. If I find out any one of you is feeding information to the press or withholding information from a fellow officer, you're out. Everyone got it?"

The officers nodded their heads, some vocalizing their assent to the chief's orders.

Next, a representative from both the State's Attorney's Office and Internal Affairs spoke. The chief went over all the findings to date—bodies, locations, evidence, areas, and officers assigned to each case. After taking a few questions the chief dismissed the meeting.

"All right everyone, get out of here and let's catch this guy."

Detective Stone unfolded his arms and glanced around the conference room. He saw some of the cops from Area Two. He walked over to find Detective Reilly, who he knew had been assigned the Jordan Nash kidnapping. Another officer pointed Reilly out and Stone walked up to him.

"Detective Jack Stone, Area Four Violent Crimes," he said and offered his hand to Reilly.

"Sam Reilly, Area Two VC." Reilly firmly shook Stone's hand.

"You're the one working with the girl who was kidnapped and brought into your shop?"

"That's right."

"It's for sure that our guy had her?"

"Forensics says so. Fibers match up with the Pilsen victims. Gray wool and blue polyester fibers were found all over her shirt."

"No kidding?"

"Nope. He had her all right."

"You think I can get copies of the girl's statement and those fiber reports?" Stone asked.

"Sure thing. She doesn't remember anything, though. The guy drugged her."

"Maybe I can talk to her?" Stone suggested.

Reilly's back stiffened and he became noticeably defensive, but remembering what the chief had just finished saying, he reluctantly agreed. "Yeah, I guess so. She doesn't recall the details of the night. It might be too early still, but I can send you the report."

"Great," Stone said, not missing Reilly's uncooperative attitude.

"And I can get copies of your reports also? On the dead women found in Pilsen? I haven't seen forensics or autopsy reports on them."

It was Stone's turn to hesitate. "When I can get to them. I'm not headed back to the station right now. But maybe tomorrow."

"Uh-huh," Reilly mumbled. "I'll give you a call. How does that sound?" Reilly offered Stone his card.

"Sounds fair. And here's mine as well," Stone replied, exchanging cards with Reilly.

"You'll be hearing from me."

"I'm sure I will," mumbled Reilly, sauntering off.

Once Reilly disappeared, Stone left the conference room and headed back to the station. He had to find those reports. He'd left them with Arnie and hadn't seen them since. He was concerned about their absence.

His partner, before leaving on suspension, asked Stone to find and destroy two arrest reports for prostitutes on whom he had recently lowered charges. Arnie didn't want IA catching up to him. Stone had refused to help him. He was still in shock that Arnie was involved in this kind of scandal.

Arnie had known it was a big favor to ask and had left it alone when Stone didn't answer right away. Stone still hadn't decided if he was going to help his long-time partner out of this mess or not. He wanted to help him, but not like this. He had told Arnie the same.

Now the autopsy and forensics reports on the dead Pilsen women were missing. Stone could get duplicates, but it would take at least several days to deal with the lab, time which he didn't have.

Stone was worried.

Arnie hadn't taken the reports, had he? He wasn't trying to stall this investigation, was he?

It was a crazy idea. He tried to erase the notion from his head. The reports were probably buried in Arnie's desk somewhere. The poor guy had been completely distraught and shook up when he left the other day. He probably misplaced them, that's all.

Stone had enough on his mind. The last thing he needed was the chief crawling up his butt over missing reports, thanks to Reilly's hassles. His head was pounding. He needed an aspirin and a drink.

And he needed to talk to this kidnapping victim, Jordan Nash.

Chapter Thirty-nine

Area Four Station
November 13
3:43 P.M.

As promised, Detective Reilly had forwarded him copies of the kidnapping victim's statement and the reports on the Beaubien Woods body. They only had autopsy reports back, no forensics, but Reilly sent the crime scene notes also.

Stone, however, was having difficulty reciprocating. He had pulled Arnie's desk apart looking for the reports on the Pilsen women and came up with nothing. He tried to call Arnie at home, to see how he was handling everything, and admittedly because he was awfully concerned over the disappearance of the Pilsen victim reports. No answer from Arnie, though, and still no return call.

Stone sat down at his own desk and leaned back in his squeaky plastic chair, resting his head against the locked palms of his raised arms.

He was concerned. Arnie had left the station quickly, understandably upset when Stone rejected his plea for help. Now Stone felt terrible, unsure whether he had made the right decision in refusing his friend. The two had worked together for years and watched one another's backs, not just on the streets. Stone had violated that trust, that reliability. But hadn't Arnie as well? Hadn't Arnie violated the unspoken code between the two with his actions? If he was guilty of accepting sexual favors from prostitutes in exchange for lowering their charges, what else was he capable of? What was wrong with him?

Stone felt frustrated and overwhelmed by all that had been thrown at him in the last few weeks. He was angry with Arnie for putting him in this position. He was working this case alone now. At the same time, he was being forced to betray either his partner or the department. However, if he didn't get Reilly some information, there wouldn't be a department to worry about.

Stone stood up from his desk and stretched. He was exhausted, worn out from the whole thing. He picked up Reilly's faxed reports once more and tried to concentrate on the investigation.

Jordan Nash hadn't remembered much. It didn't appear that she would be able to provide them with much help. He decided to back off and let Reilly continue to work with her.

Stone also perused the crime scene notes from the Beaubien Woods victim. The girl had been found naked, near the river's edge, and like the others, carved into and left with a makeshift noose around her neck. The evidence technician had pulled something from under her nails that looked like a piece of tape, the crime scene notes said. The sample had been sent to forensics, although no report was back on the item yet.

Forensics had informed Area Two the girl's body was found near a patch of purple looseleaf, a purple flowering plant common in Beaubien Woods, although rare in the rest of Illinois.

Stone sighed. They had so little to go on. Dead bodies kept turning up and it didn't seem like he was getting any closer. The killer was growing more aggressive with each victim. Who was next?

And was this guy really a cop, like Jordan Nash said? If so, there were 14,000 cops, several hundred detectives; where would he begin?

Book V

Upholding
the Law

Chapter Forty

Janna spent most of her afternoon researching a possible consent defense for her newest client, the charming doctor. The outlook was not so good. In Illinois, if there was a trust relationship between two people, like a doctor and a patient, the fact that the patient consented to examination was irrelevant. For legal purposes, a patient could not consent to an improper examination.

Janna would have to stick with the insanity approach, which meant she needed to prove her client was unable to appreciate the wrongness of his actions

227

at the time. She could argue the assault took place during a seizure or a fit. It would be tougher than she originally thought, but her options were few.

She turned the computer off and prepared to go home for the night. She found herself thinking about Jack Stone, for what felt like the hundredth time that day. She couldn't keep her mind off their date, and although she felt like a foolish teenager, she wanted to get home early to see if he had called.

Smiling to herself, she walked out to the main entrance, where she was surprised to find Kelsey Dore. She was standing in the middle of the waiting area. As usual, the secretary was missing from her desk.

"Janna Scott, right?" Kelsey recognized Janna as the woman who had cross-examined her the other day.

"Yes. You're Kelsey Dore. You shouldn't be here," Janna told her quickly.

"I shouldn't be a lot of places, like on the witness stand at the damn courthouse, or named as a defendant in a civil lawsuit by your perverted old man client," Kelsey almost shouted.

"This is not the place for this kind of outburst, Ms. Dore." Janna glanced around the reception area, knowing other attorneys were still working and hoping no one could hear them.

"Your client is stalking me. Do you know that? Do you know about this lawsuit he filed?" Kelsey was shouting now and waving a piece of paper in the air. "I'm supposed to file an answer, this paper says. Well, I'm here to file it with you!" Kelsey bellowed. "My answer is that your client is pure scum, absolute filth! I can't believe you can look at yourself in the mirror every morning knowing you represent a rapist!"

The young woman was visibly shaken. She lowered her voice and the two women locked eyes. Without flinching, Kelsey said, "Maybe he'll come after you next. Maybe then you'll know what it's like."

"I understand you're upset, but—"

"You tell that freak to stay away from me!"

Kelsey was upset and distraught. In fact, the young blonde seemed close to tears. Janna tried to calm her down or at least remove her from the shared reception area.

"I'm not responsible for the filing of any civil lawsuit against you. I didn't even know about it. You'll have to file a written answer, though, on the seventh floor of the Daley Center," Jana offered.

"I don't need any help from you. Just tell him to stay away from me!" Kelsey looked at Janna with pure hatred.

Janna felt more bothered than she cared to admit. She wasn't used to this kind of treatment, not from a victim. She had served as a victim's advocate for so long. It was strange to be on the other side.

Kelsey dug her heels into the ground and spun herself around, storming out of the small waiting area. Janna was speechless, stunned by the young woman's harsh remarks, and strongly doubting her client. She needed to talk with him. If he had filed a lawsuit on his own, he had gone too far. And was he stalking Kelsey? The sick feeling in her stomach told her the answer, but she could be wrong. She wanted to back out of this case, but first she had to talk to her client.

Chapter Forty-one

Cook County Hospital, Jail Section
November 13
6:13 P.M.

James's cough could have been heard two units away, Sarah thought. His body seemed to convulse with each sputter from his mouth. A gurgling noise was coming from deep in his throat. Sarah hurried over to his bedside, and was horrified by what she found.

James's chest and chin were covered in blood. She lifted his sheet to check the rest of his body. With relief, she noticed his body looked okay. His chest filled and he lifted his torso off the bed and heaved out a bloody mass right onto Sarah's shirt sleeve. He was coughing up a lot of blood.

Sarah worked hurriedly, pressing the call button next to him. She needed to get more staff members in the room. He would have to be moved back to ICU. His heart monitor line was flashing by, a series of sporadic peaks. James's health was faltering, and seriously.

"Hang in there," she encouraged the unconscious man lying in front of her. "Sarah is going to make sure you're safe, mister. That's a promise."

She prepared him for transport. There was no telling what was going on with him.

Two nurses came to her aid and removed James from the section. His eyes had lolled back into his head and his body was shaking.

What had happened so suddenly, she wondered? He was healing so beautifully, his speech slowly returning. Now this. A complete setback in his progress, or so it seemed. Maybe the doctors would say otherwise, she hoped. One thing was certain, he wouldn't be transferred out of Cook County in this condition. He'd be stabilized and brought back down to her, for at least a couple of weeks. If he even could be stabilized, she thought.

Sarah had grown fond of James, more so than she had expected, and hoped he would pull through.

"It's too bad. He was starting to come around. I swear I almost had him back," she said to the empty room.

She wondered if he had any family or friends in the area. No one had called about his progress or tried to visit him. He just lay there, all alone in the world. Poor man. Never even knew what happened to him. Just got whacked and wound up here.

Well, if ICU could stabilize him, she would be happy to take him back. Sarah had made James her pet project. She could pull him through this, if the hospital would just give her enough time.

Chapter Forty-two

The Soldier of Death walked quietly behind the nun, falling back into the shadows, remaining out of sight. Sister Fitzgerald was her name. She had been speaking in Chicago about the plight of some of her fellow missionary sisters in various parts of the world. She claimed the nuns were being abused by priests. Nuns in third-world countries were reportedly being raped by some of the priests who were afraid to use the local prostitutes, due to how widespread AIDS was.

The sisters' tales of woe were picked up by the *Tribune* and reports of abuse from around the world flooded into the paper. Sister Fitzgerald was creating waves in the Catholic community. The sister had just left Holy Name Cathedral and was on her way to meet a friend who was studying at the Moody Bible Institute a few blocks away.

The Soldier of Death followed her quietly, never losing sight of her habit, bobbing up and down in front of him. He had read the article in the *Tribune* earlier that week and had become enraged at the nun's blasphemy and with her actions. How dare she speak out against the church? He had come for her. She had spoken ill of the church and thus, of God. By his hand, she must die. It was the only way. He was only acting as God's messenger.

He was the Chosen One and she was just another one of the Intended. He picked up his pace as the sister cut across Bughouse Square, using the diagonal sidewalk. She was passing in front of the Newberry Library. The Soldier of Death held his breath as he fell into step right behind her.

Sister Fitzgerald came to the edge of the park and stepped out of the lights and into the dark shadows of the street. The Soldier saw his opportunity and pounced. He grabbed the petite woman from behind, covering her mouth with his gloved hand, his other arm locked around her waist. She didn't have a chance to scream. He dragged her down the street about half a block, her legs flailing, thrashing out at the empty air.

The alley was only a half block from the park and was dark and quiet. The Soldier pulled the nun into the alley and threw her up against a brick wall. Her head hit the wall hard. He pressed his forearm against her neck, cutting off her air supply and holding her firmly against the building.

Her eyes widened with fear as she stared him straight in the face, knowing she was about to meet her final fate. The Soldier knew he needed to do this, or God would not clear his own path. He would bring His wrath down on the Soldier.

He reached up with his left hand and bashed the nun's skull against the wall. He felt a tingle of excitement ripple down his spine. He let go of the woman's neck and her limp body crumpled to the ground. She was still alive, although unconscious.

The Soldier dragged her across the alley toward a large Dumpster. He reached down and wrapped his fingers around the nun's throat, squeezing, gently at first, then much harder. He squeezed the nun's last breath from her. Then, he pulled a rope from his belt loops and tied it around her throat.

"You won't have so much to say now, will you Sister?"

The Soldier had completed his task, done his duty. He removed the cross from around the woman's neck and pressed it into her open palm, closing her fingers tightly around the symbol. He said a prayer over her lifeless body.

"Hail Mary, blessed are thou. Holy Mary, blessed is the fruit of thy womb, Jesus . . ."

His prayers were abruptly halted when he was startled by a pair of approaching headlights. Although still blocks away, the car was coming down the alley.

236

The Soldier stopped and heaved the nun's body into the Dumpster. He slammed the lid shut. His job here was done. He couldn't get caught up in the aftermath. He had listened and obeyed. Now God would take care of him. He trotted off, ducking around the corner as the headlights neared.

A rush of energy pulsed through his body, his veins throbbing. He felt as if he would explode. He hadn't felt this fulfilled in the past. This one had felt especially good.

Each time, each victim, had to be more grandiose than the last. He had to prove he was worthy of more. The Soldier of Death disappeared into the street's dark pockets and thought about his next victim, hoping he would be summoned soon.

Chapter Forty-three

The Chief of Detectives heard another body had been discovered in the 18th district, in an alley. The kicker was the police station was directly at the end of the alley. The killer basically left the body on their doorstep. This time he grabbed a nun, strangled her, and left her in a Dumpster. Her throat, like the others, was bound by a rope tied in a Celtic knot.

The latest victim was clearly meant to send them another message. The Cross-Town Killer had taken religious symbolism to a whole new level. A nun? He was definitely nuts, which made the CPD's job a lot tougher.

The only bright point was the killer had grown not only angrier, but sloppier. This time he hadn't left the victim in a pool of water. They might be able to recover more trace evidence from her corpse than they had gotten from the other victims.

The chief didn't like that this guy was now working the Gold Coast. This latest killing gave a whole new meaning to the press's nickname, "Cross-Town Killer." The guy was not only carving crosses into the bodies of these women, but he was crossing the city with his victim choice, covering all walks of life from prostitutes to nuns, from the North Side to the South Side. The chief cleared his throat. Exasperated, he called out to his deputy.

"Jody, let's get Jack Stone from Area Four VC on the phone. Conference call him."

Within minutes, the chief had Stone on the line.

"What's going on with this thing? The press and the mayor will have my ass on a silver platter if we don't get this guy. Have you guys got anything new on those Pilsen women?"

"No, we don't. But I heard the latest on the news this morning. A nun, huh? Garbage collectors found her?"

"That's right. She was coming from Holy Name. This is getting beyond ugly, Stone."

"You don't need to tell me that. Problem is, his victim type keeps changing. We don't know who he's going to grab next."

"Well, someone better damn figure it out!" the chief yelled. "I need to give the people of this city some answers, starting with the Mayor's Office. They've already called twice this morning."

"We're mainly working off the profile we got from the forensic psychologist. Trying to do a run-down on potential suspects. The profiler thinks the guy might be in law enforcement. Someone educated with technical skills. The kidnapping victim claims the guy said he was a homicide detective. He could have been lying, though."

"I thought you said the killer was educated? That should leave out most law enforcement personnel, shouldn't it? You shouldn't have any trouble narrowing it down."

The chief was angry. He didn't mean to take his hostility out on Stone, but he needed a suspect. This city wouldn't accept his coming up empty-handed.

"Stone, you bring someone in on this. I don't care how you do it, just do it soon." The chief slammed down the phone.

Why hadn't Stone found someone for him already? Why hadn't these guys pulled anyone in? The mayor was going to be breathing down his neck for sure this time. A Holy Name nun? This would definitely not sit well in the community. He loosened his shirt collar and rolled up his sleeves for what was sure to be a long day.

What could be worse than killing a nun?

The chief had a sickening feeling in his stomach that he was about to find out.

Chapter Forty-four

Reilly's hunch paid off. He knew the sample would match. Well, not match exactly, but the source was identified. Detective Reilly asked the crime lab technicians to compare the blue fibers taken from Jordan Nash's oxford to fibers taken from a 1999 Chevy Caprice seat, the car most detectives drove. He also asked the crime lab to compare the gray fibers against those taken from a gray wool, standard-issue police blanket, the kind most cops kept in their trunk.

While it was not an exact match—the dye patterns

differed—the lab report verified it was a high probability both sets of fibers came from a similar source. This meant the fibers found on Jordan Nash could have come from another Caprice Classic and blanket.

This meant the guy could be a cop, like Jordan Nash said. Could the killer really be one of their own? Another copper? Could he actually be using the department's car to move these bodies, to grab these women?

Reilly needed to talk to the commander. They would have to get Internal Affairs involved if a cop was suspected. He couldn't just start questioning the other officers.

Reilly also needed to ask the commander about Stone. Stone still hadn't forwarded the autopsy reports from the Pilsen victims, and he had been acting strangely when the two spoke on the phone, almost as if he was hiding something. Reilly didn't trust him. He had asked a lot of questions about Jordan Nash. He'd seemed overeager to talk to the girl and then backed off suddenly. It was odd.

The chief said any misconduct or refusal to cooperate would be severely disciplined, but he didn't want to rat Stone out. He'd get a bad name around the department. Maybe he shouldn't say anything about Stone at all. Besides, who needed his help anyway?

If Reilly could crack this case on his own he'd be on his way up in no time. He'd be flying through the ranks. Reilly would be a hero, and if Stone didn't want to help him, fine. He didn't plan on doing him any favors either. Every man for himself, if that's how he wanted to play—so be it.

Chapter Forty-five

Metzenstein Rare Coin and Stamp Dealers
212 North Clark Street
November 14
10:42 A.M.

The mayor's daughter, Noreen Gallagher, looked up from the window display case she was working on when the customer came into the shop. Noreen, or Norie, as friends and family called her, was eight months' pregnant. Her large belly was causing her trouble as she tried to position several valuable coins in a window.

Norie was an expert in rare coins and stamps, and the exclusive Loop dealer held some of the rarest and most valuable in both categories. Noreen had been an Art History major in college and enjoyed the stimulating work of caring for such small, detailed items. She had recently married and the newlyweds were now expecting their first child together.

"Hello, can I help you, sir?" she asked the handsome stranger.

"Yes, I'm looking for a World War II–era German stamp, something to complement my collection," the man said.

"Fabulous. We have a couple of things I can show you." She paused for a minute, tilting her head and squinting at the man. "Don't I know you? Have you been in before?" she asked.

"I have, but not in a long while. You're Noreen Gallagher, aren't you?"

"That's right. You can call me Norie, though." She smiled. His recognition didn't exactly surprise her. Pictures from her wedding had been splashed throughout Chicago's society pages and, as the mayor's daughter, she often made public appearances.

"I know your father," the man told her.

"Doesn't everyone?" Norie laughed.

"I suppose so. But I meant that I live down the block from him. He's attended a couple of parties at my home."

"Oh! No wonder you look familiar. You're one of my parents' neighbors."

"Dr. Mason Von Patton." The man extended his hand.

"Nice to meet you."

"And you as well. Now, about those stamps . . ."

"Certainly."

Norie showed the doctor several stamps from the era and the two chatted amicably about the tedious task of stamp collecting. The doctor purchased a 1933 stamp from her.

"Do you sell hinges by any chance?"

Stamp hinges were translucent pre-glued materials used to affix stamps to the pages of collector books.

"Not for this beautiful stamp!" Norie was horrified.

The doctor chuckled. "No, for some of my lesser-quality collecribles."

"Oh, of course." Norie's face flushed with embarassment. She sighed, relieved the doctor wasn't planning to hinge his new stamp. "We don't sell them here. Down the street in the Marquette building. There's a shop in there."

"I'll try that." The doctor thanked her for her gracious assistance and took his package from her.

"It's been a true pleasure." He smiled at her kindly. "Say hello to your father for me."

"I'll be sure to do that," Norie said, smiling back at the charming man.

Chapter Forty-six

19 South LaSalle
November 14
11:12 A.M.

Janna read the front page of the *Tribune* with disgust. The headlines screamed in anger over the killing of a nun. The nun's body was found in an alley, not far from Janna's office. She read through the story and the reporter's conclusion that not only was a serial killer on the loose in the city, but thus far, the police department's efforts had proved almost entirely fruitless. There were already five victims. Janna shook her head. People were really sick, she thought.

She put the paper down and reached for her Caribou coffee when Dr. Von Patton came through her door.

"How did you get back here? Didn't the secretary

out front stop you?" Janna asked him, annoyed by the sudden intrusion.

"There was no one out there."

Janna shook her head. "Figures," she mumbled. "You don't have an appointment."

"I was in the neighborhood. Thought I'd drop in and see how things were coming."

"Really? Coming from the Daley Center?" Janna asked, with raised eyebrows.

"No. Metzenstein's Rare Stamps and Coins. Across the street. I collect stamps. Why?"

"Your patient paid me a visit the other day, Kelsey Dore."

"Did she?" he smiled lasciviously.

"She did. She says you're following her around, stalking her."

The doctor snorted, seemingly amused by the proposition. "That's absurd. She's obviously a completely paranoid and delusional young woman."

"Nonetheless, if you have been trying to intimidate Miss Dore in any way, I needn't remind you how bad it would look at trial if you are caught."

The doctor leaned back in the worn guest chair and rolled his eyes. "She'll go to all extremes it seems. To ruin me, that is."

"She said you filed a civil lawsuit against her?"

"That's right. I filed it myself."

"Without counsel?"

"Without counsel. I think you attorneys have done more than enough for me already."

"I see." Janna braced herself in her chair, ready for another confrontation with her client. This guy was turning out to be a total nutcase, she thought. "About your insanity defense . . ." If the shoe fit, he might as well wear it, she thought.

"Yes, about that. Do you think you are going to be able to prove it?"

"I am going to argue your actions took place during an epileptic seizure, if at all, and that you have no recollection of any of the events these women are testifying about."

"Perfect. And completely true, I might add."

"Which means I will need to see those records. Whatever Dr. Shore has. She tells me you haven't filled out a release yet, is that right?"

"I completely forgot. I'm sorry." The doctor stood up to leave.

"Please do it as soon as you can," Janna asked.

"Sure. I'll see if she has anything in her files about the seizures and have her send it over to you right away. I'll call her now."

"I need the whole file. Not just what she has about the seizures. I need to figure out why the State is trying to access those records and how to protect them."

"The State?" Dr. Von Patton turned back, on his way out the door.

"Yes, the State. They sent someone over to talk to Dr. Shore."

"And?"

"And she didn't tell them anything."

"Oh." The doctor seemed surprised. "Won't you have to give the materials to the State anyway? During discovery?"

"Yes, if we use Dr. Shore in your defense. But certain things will be subject to the doctor-patient privilege."

"Isn't that marvelous?" the doctor said sarcastically.

"If you say so."

Dr. Von Patton left Janna's office, whistling loudly as he walked down the hallway.

"What a character," she said to the empty room after he was gone. She picked the newspaper back up to finish reading the front page.

Chapter Forty-seven

City Memorial Hospital
November 14
12:41 P.M.

Dr. Von Patton felt slightly better once he entered the research lab. His assistant had been on vacation for the past several days, so the lab was empty. Here, amid his research, he was comfortable. His attorney had run his nerves over a grater. His fuse shortened, he knew it was best if he concentrated on his work.

Before leaving her office, Janna had asked him to call his psychiatrist again. Not a chance. Those were his personal medical records, his private conversations with his doctor. He wasn't about to release them to Janna. So she could give them to the State's Attorney during the discovery process? So some judge could pry through them? No thanks. He was smarter than that.

Janna would find another doctor to testify on his behalf. She would have to. He was not about to make his past mental health and medical records part of a very public record. Not to mention the risk of losing his license. Coupled with the public shaming of the whole experience, it was too much to bear.

Dr. Von Patton went over to the locked storage container and removed the blood samples from several of his HIV patients. Using protective wear, he prepared a glass slide from some of the blood and placed it under the electric microscope.

The doctor was studying a mutated form of HIV that seemed to be multiplying among Cook County Jail inmates. The mutated strand didn't respond to the regular treatment methods and had proven immensely resilient. It also developed faster. A patient infected with the mutated virus would reach full-blown AIDS within two years of diagnosis. It was fascinating.

Dr. Von Patton studied the slide for a few moments, but soon found his hands shaking. His eyes would not focus. He was sweating. He had to stop this cycle. He couldn't take much more. His body was breaking down.

Maybe he should take the plea, he thought. The problem with the plea was that it not only guaranteed him a record, but it also forced him to register as a sex offender. He would ruin both his medical practice and his good name. It was not a practical solution.

Extremely frustrated, he knew his breaking point had been punctured. His patience was trickling out, disappearing through an illusionary hole. His nerves had shattered under the pressure.

His entire life was hanging in the so-called balance of justice, and this woman, Janna, didn't seem to care. To her, he was just another client, another faceless name for her to push along through the system.

He pulled off the gloves he was wearing and left the lab area, feeling as if he was about to vomit. His stomach churned and lurched. Maybe the fresh air would help. He took the mail that had been pushed underneath the lab door and went outside, forgetting to lock up the blood samples.

Once outside, he gulped in the cool air, breathing deeply, allowing the lake wind to blow against his face. He tried to stop his hands from shaking. He was still holding the mail.

He sat down on a nearby metal bench and tried to relax. He sorted through the mail, trying to focus on the small task, and still dry heaving. A bill for the lab space had come. One more thing he didn't need.

He hadn't secured funding from NIH yet. If he didn't finish his research, he wasn't going to secure it either. He had only a little further to go and his paper would be done. He needed to get rid of this ridiculous criminal case against him. He planned to do everything in his power to insure his usual output, a hit. He wanted to make waves and set the infectious disease community abuzz. And he would go to hell before he let Kelsey Dore stop him.

Just a little further and he would have it. He knew what he had to do, and soon.

Chapter Forty-eight

1918 South Indiana
November 18
6:07 P.M.

Kelsey and Jeff slowly pulled up to the address they had been given by the operator.

"Is that it?" Kelsey asked.

"It's gotta be. It's the only 1918 on the block. They said South Indiana."

"It doesn't look like anyone's home."

"I'm going to try the doorbell. You wait here."

"You don't need to tell me twice," Kelsey replied.

Jeff turned off his car lights and parked on the street. He left the engine running, so Kelsey could have heat and just in case he needed to get out of there quickly. He approached the gray stone home carefully, glancing back over his shoulder at the car.

On the front porch, he peered in the narrow windows next to the large door. They were covered by sheer drapes, but Jeff could see through them a bit. He could see there was no one in the front rooms of the house. He rang the doorbell.

He heard a loud chime clang through the house. He waited for several minutes. No one came to the door. He rang the bell again. Still no answer.

He glanced back over his shoulder once more. Kelsey was watching from the passenger seat of his car. He shrugged his shoulders and held his hands up, mouthing "No one's home." She motioned for him to come back to the car.

Jeff trotted over to the car and got in beside his girlfriend.

"No one's home. He's not answering the doorbell."

"He's probably still working. I knew we shouldn't have come this early."

"You didn't want to come at all, what are you talking about?"

"I'm here, aren't I? I meant . . . I just knew we should have come later, that's all."

Suddenly, a car's bright lights reflected into Jeff's eyes from his rearview mirror. Someone was approaching. Kelsey turned to see who was nearing them. She recognized the car at once.

"That's him. And that's the car. I swear it, Jeff. That

was the car that followed me on campus the other day."

"All right. I believe you, just wait here."

Jeff waited for Dr. Von Patton to pull into his driveway and turn his engine off. The doctor opened his car door and seemed to be collecting some items from the backseat. Jeff emerged from his own car and approached the doctor quietly, tapping him on the shoulder while he was still digging in the backseat.

"Excuse me, Dr. Von Patton?"

The doctor seemed startled. He turned around cautiously.

"Yes, can I help you?"

"I'm Jeff Gordon, Kelsey Dore's boyfriend."

"Get out of here. Get off my property," the doctor said angrily.

"Stay away from her then. Don't make me come back here."

Jeff took several steps toward the doctor, shoving his large football player chest into the doctor's face. He glared down at Dr. Von Patton. He hadn't planned to be so confrontational, but the trembling doctor was making it too easy.

"I'm going to call the police," Dr. Von Patton blurted.

"Go ahead. We already have. I'm sure they'll rush right over here to help you out," Jeff sneered. He hated the sniveling man before him. This man who had caused both he and Kelsey so much trouble and heartache.

Jeff didn't back away. He watched as the doctor grabbed his things from the car seat and slammed the door.

"I'm watching you, Dr. Von Patton. You don't fool us."

"Does your girlfriend know she's supposed to avoid contact with me?" the doctor said arrogantly, threatening Jeff.

"I'm not my girlfriend, am I?"

"Please leave," the doctor said again, brushing past Jeff timidly and walking toward his house. Jeff watched him enter the house, then returned to Kelsey, still waiting in the car.

"If he bothers you again, I swear I'll pummel him," Jeff said.

"What did he say?"

"He's still denying it. He'll leave you alone, though. I promise."

Jeff pulled the car away from the curb and drove back up to Loyola's campus. From inside, Dr. Von Patton watched them pull away, his gaze following the car until it finally disappeared around a corner.

Chapter Forty-nine

Jordan had been working with the police sketch artist for the past two hours. The composite was just starting to look familiar to her. After visiting the hypnotherapist, her anxiety had decreased while her memory of the event increased. At first, she had only vaguely recalled her attacker's face. But piece by piece, her memory was becoming stronger on its own.

She returned to the police station and told Detective Reilly she had been remembering certain aspects, minute details, from the kidnapping. She hadn't told him about the therapist.

Detective Reilly came over to her and the sketch artist to check on their progress.

"Does that look like the guy?" Reilly asked.

"Yeah, but . . . I don't know. Something's not right. I can't figure it out. The nose doesn't look quite right."

"Do you want to keep working?"

Jordan was tired. Although feeling better, she still suffered from sleepless nights and tension. Today she had a dull headache that threatened to worsen if she didn't lie down soon.

"I think I'm going to go home. The picture looks good so far. I'll take a copy with me and think about it some more. Maybe tomorrow it will be clearer. Sorry, but I have to take a break." Jordan's eyes were apologetic.

"Okay. Go home, get some rest. We don't want to put any pressure on you. Come back when you're ready."

Detective Reilly had been supportive and patient from the start. She was grateful he was assigned to her case.

"Let's make a couple copies of the sketch," Reilly told the artist. "You can always add to it, change it, right?"

"Sure," the sketch artist replied.

"Okay."

The sketch artist handed Reilly the drawing of the kidnapper, at least as much of him as Jordan could remember. Reilly made a copy for himself and Jordan and returned the original to the artist.

"I'm going to hold off on distributing this until you come back in, tomorrow or the next day, okay? Unless you're sure, then I'll get this thing out there."

"No. Just wait. I know I can remember more. Give me until tomorrow. It's coming back slowly. I can't be totally sure right now, but maybe after another night's sleep," Jordan promised.

"Fine. Anything else?"

"I am going to my hypnotherapist soon. Maybe I should wait until after that to finish the sketch," she suggested.

"Your what?" Detective Reilly asked.

"My hypnotherapist. He's using hypnosis to help me cope with this whole thing. One of the side effects is my sharpened memory of the incident."

"Oh, great." Reilly sighed, obviously disappointed by her news.

"What's wrong?" Jordan asked.

"If you're going to a hypnotist, you're not going to be able to testify about this guy. The courts won't allow hypnosis-enhanced testimony," Reilly said.

"Well, I can still help you catch the guy, right? You do want to catch him, don't you?"

"Yeah, but trying him is a whole other story."

"I wouldn't remember anything if it weren't for the hypnosis. With or without it, I would have been useless in court," she insisted. "At least this way you can get some information from me."

"That's true," Reilly agreed. "Just be sure before you give me any new information though, okay? This kind of thing can blow a whole case."

"You got it. But I swear to you, everything I've remembered so far, I'm sure of it, one hundred percent."

"All right, fine. I'm holding the sketch, though." He stuffed the sketch into his breast pocket, clearly doubting the accuracy of her memory.

"Agreed, for now."

Jordan shook the detective's hand and left the station. She knew what she was doing, even if the police didn't believe her. And if they wanted to catch this killer, they had no choice but to believe her.

Book VI

The Rabbit Hunter

Chapter Fifty

Stone had it with the chief. He was on his ass for no reason. Stone was working sixteen hours a day trying to catch the Cross-Town Killer. What more did the chief want? Did he want him to just go out and arrest someone? Anyone to keep the mayor happy? Obviously, the chief was catching crap from someone at the top, and it was rolling downhill quickly. And Stone was standing at the bottom of that hill, buried in it.

Sylvia, the desk clerk, came by to talk to him. "How's it going?"

"Ah, not so great. We don't have squat on this guy."

"Don't they think he's a cop?"

"Nah, I don't even know about that. That's what the kidnapping victim says, but he could have been lying to her. Regardless, there are a lot of cops in this city, if he even is a cop."

"Don't I know it?" Sylvia folded her arms and leaned up against the doorframe. "Who do you think talks to them all day long?" She examined her fingernails for a minute. "The chief's got it out for you, doesn't he?"

"Yeah, thanks for the reminder. What do I have? A few dead prostitutes, no eye witnesses, no suspects, and a profile that seems to change with each victim. Maybe I should just go arrest some beat cop, drag him in here for questioning."

Sylvia laughed. "That reminds me of a joke. You want to hear it?"

Stone looked up from his paperwork. "Sure, shoot."

"Okay. A rabbit robs a liquor store and kills the clerk. The rabbit runs into a forest. The CIA, the ATF, and the CPD are all investigating. The CIA conducts a series of advanced tests on the forest and the wildlife. What do they conclude?"

"What?"

"The rabbit doesn't exist."

Stone snickered.

"The ATF goes in and torches the whole forest. Nothing's left, demolished. They figure, hey, at least we got the rabbit, right?"

"Right," he chuckled. "And the CPD?"

"The CPD goes into the forest, they grab a bear,

beat the crap out of it until it runs out shouting, 'I'm a rabbit! I'm a rabbit!'"

Stone howled. "Isn't that the truth!"

"Thought I'd make you laugh." Sylvia smiled from the doorway.

"You did. Thanks, Sylvia. Now, I guess I better get out there and go find the chief a bear."

"Go catch us a big one," she said, before returning to the front reception area.

"I will. That's a promise."

Stone put his paperwork away and decided to go over to Internal Affairs. It wouldn't hurt to check on Arnie's case. He had a friend over there. He could also get a list of CPD detectives from personnel. He had to start somewhere.

On his way out he couldn't help thinking about Janna. He knew he didn't have much time for a personal life these days, but she had really gotten to him. Her strawberry blond hair, green eyes, and her long, slender body. Stone also liked her spunk. And she was smart too. He talked to her on the phone the other night and wanted to see her again.

But first, first he had a rabbit to catch. Screw the chief and his pressure tactics. He wasn't bringing anyone in unless he had the right guy.

Chapter Fifty-one

The State filed a motion to have Dr. Mason Von Patton declared a Sexually Dangerous Person, pursuant to the Sexually Dangerous Persons Act. In other words, the State was seeking to have the doctor declared a sex predator and have him stuffed into a mental hospital until they determined him rehabilitated. Go straight to jail and don't pass go.

This meant two things to Janna. One, her client was most likely lying to her about his past arrest record. And two, it provided an explanation as to why the State was trying to get information from Dr. Shore.

Janna was fuming. The doctor had been dishonest

with her from the start. He had lied to her, been difficult to work with, and had flat out insulted and offended her on several occasions. What had she been thinking when she decided to do criminal defense work anyway?

The doctor's hearing was only a couple of weeks away, which gave her little time for preparation. The State had to prove that Von Patton exhibited a propensity to commit sexual acts of an offensive nature. A propensity required more than the doctor's current act, much more.

"What are you hiding, Dr. Von Patton? What didn't you tell me?" Janna said aloud to her computer screen.

She still had a friend in the FBI LEADS department at 26th and California. He would run a background check for her if she asked him. Since her client wasn't telling her the truth, that was her only alternative. She wasn't planning on showing up at court unprepared. No, this time she would find out for herself, without asking the doctor.

One thing she didn't have time for was another lying sex offender. If Von Patton wanted a defense, she needed the facts, and she needed them now.

There was a chance the State was just throwing more wood on the fire, hoping to back the doctor into a plea. But Janna had a bad feeling that wasn't the case. Her client had a past. She had sensed it initially. She just didn't know what it was. Not yet.

Chapter Fifty-two

1918 South Indiana
November 15
3:26 P.M.

Dr. Von Patton ripped the phone from the kitchen wall jack after he finished listening to his voice mail. He had been unable to sleep last night and had come home early, exhausted. Now this.

What the hell was the Sexually Dangerous Persons Act? What was Janna talking about?

Janna said he must have something in his past, a previous arrest or conviction if the State was seeking to have him declared a Sexually Dangerous Person. If he was declared as such, he would be locked away for "treatment," she said.

I don't think so, Ms. Scott. No one's getting rid of me that easily.

He had worked far too hard to let these hags start tinkering with his life now. Janna Scott, Dr. Shore, Kelsey Dore, all of them were in for a big surprise if they thought he was going to quietly disappear into some damn asylum.

He cracked his knuckles repeatedly, pacing back and forth across the terra-cotta tiled floor. He had done everything he was supposed to: took his medication, visited his psychiatrist, prayed for the urges to stop. And yet he was in the same position again, the same scenario from years before. Only this time, it was worse.

This time, he really didn't remember touching these women, harming them. And this time he had a past, a record that would make him appear guilty as hell if it ever came to light.

Janna said the State would move to have a court appointed psychiatrist evaluate him. They may try to have Dr. Shore's records released as well, to try and dig up any past "sexual propensities." Janna thought this might be helpful, if Shore's records were devoid of anything incriminating.

Sorry, Janna. Wrong again.

Dr. Von Patton knew the release of those records would mean his instant demise in the medical community, in his private life, everywhere. Those records proved anything but his innocence. He couldn't let it happen. These women had to be stopped before they destroyed him. It was his last resort. It sounded as if his past conviction had already been discovered by the State. They were already on to him.

Janna would be angry when she learned he had lied about his past record. Tough. That was her job, wasn't it? To get him off. To deal with these types of things when they arose? He wasn't going to spoon feed her information.

He couldn't worry about her, though. His first priority was to get his records out of Dr. Shore's office.

But how? He hadn't been to see her in weeks. He had been skipping his appointments. He couldn't schedule an appointment for the sake of stealing his records. She would know he was the thief for sure.

Dr. Von Patton knew that Shore usually left her office to use the restroom before his regular appointment, right after the lunch hour. He would often see her exiting before his appointment. He assumed she probably left her office unlocked.

If he went to her office at his usual appointment time, he could wait until she left to use the restroom. He could linger around outside in the hall, unseen. Then when she walked away from the door, toward the restroom, he could slip in through the waiting area and back to her office.

He would have only a few minutes to retrieve his records, but that was all he needed. He knew exactly where she kept his file. He could take his and several other patients, that way she wouldn't know who had taken them, or if she had misplaced them herself.

Chapter Fifty-three

Cook County Hospital
November 15
4:02 P.M.

Sarah finished checking on her patients and went back to the small desk, inside the Jail Section. The phone was ringing.

"Hello?"

"Yes, this is the Jail Section."

Sarah listened for several seconds.

"Yes, we have James Johannis here. He was just released out of ICU. He's been at the hospital for several weeks. Don't you have it in your system?"

"Uh huh, I see," Sarah said as she listened to the explanation from the officer over at the county jail.

Sarah hung up the phone, annoyed. Apparently,

James had been lost in the jail's system for weeks. Prisoners often were lost in the system during routine transfers, transfers made to break up gang activity. This was ridiculous, though. For several weeks they had James listed as an escapee, after he jumped out of the courthouse window. They were just tracking him down now. Sadly enough, it was not surprising.

Sarah sighed. It wasn't her fault. She sent a daily list to the jail, reporting the inmates they had at the hospital. If they were only figuring it out now, that was their problem.

She bit her nails for a second, thinking about the errands she needed to run later. She looked at the patient list on her desk and walked back through the Jail Section, to James's curtained-off area.

"My, my, my, aren't you popular, Mr. Johannis? A couple of people have called looking for you today."

James didn't move, his eyes staring straight up at the ceiling.

"Now, I know you can hear me. You're just being modest," Sarah joked as she propped up the pillow beneath his head.

"That was the jail calling. Apparently one of the doctors over there is looking for you. A Dr. Von Patton? You know him, James? Says you're one of his HIV patients." Sarah picked up his chart and flipped through the pages. "But that's not what it says here. You're no AIDS patient. They must have you confused with someone else."

James's eyes seemed to widen, his fists clenched around the sheet his hand was wrapped through.

"Are you awake? Can you hear me?" Sarah asked, leaning in to try and peer into his eyes.

No response.

"That's not the first person to call for you today. A detective called earlier, wanted to know if you were coherent. He wanted to interview you or something. Wanted to check you out. I told him that you weren't coherent and that wasn't the policy 'round here anyway. Used to be officers could show up and just sign jail patients out if they were in good condition, for questioning and that sort of thing. No more, though, Mr. Johannis. No siree."

Sarah whistled as she adjusted James's bed, trying to put him in a comfortable position. As she tilted his bed downward and tried to face him toward the television, he winced.

"Are you awake? What's going on with you, son?" She leaned in over him.

James batted his eyes, a flicker of light dashed through his pupils, and he started to cough and sputter.

Chapter Fifty-four

19 South LaSalle
November 16
10:48 A.M.

Janna was extremely frustrated. Everything out of Dr.
Von Patton's mouth was either a lie or a severe distortion of the truth. One thing was certain, it was non-
stop action with him. She ran her fingers through her
hair and leaned back in her chair. This man was definitely making her earn her money.

Her friend from LEADS ran a background check on
her client using his date of birth and his social security
number. It seemed the doctor had been awfully busy.
He had not only one past arrest, but several. Although
he had changed his name, the FBI files had linked him
to his previous name, Terrence Thorn. Did he actually

think they wouldn't? It was only a question of time before his past caught up with him. Who did he think he was kidding?

Janna had gone down to the courthouse and retrieved the old case files from when he was previously prosecuted. She was infuriated with him. Several years ago, he had been arrested for showing naked photos of the male anatomy to young females, harassing them.

From what Janna had read, it seemed while volunteering with young students, the doctor strayed from his purpose and began to "tutor" young females one-on-one. Under the pretense that he was helping these girls, the private sessions became sexually suggestive. One of the girls told her parents and the doctor was arrested. After that, he must have changed his name.

What's next, Dr. Von Patton? Are we going to have your old girlfriend turn up buried in your backyard? Surely there must be more, Janna thought cynically.

The prognosis didn't seem to be in her client's favor. He obviously did not function well when entrusted with the care of young women. Or any women, for that matter. The doctor's rap sheet also showed a couple of arrests for the solicitation of prostitutes.

No wonder he didn't want to plead guilty. No wonder he had been against her calling character witnesses. It all made sense now. If she went to trial and called character witnesses, the State would slaughter him, tear him apart with his prior convictions. And with his priors, the State wouldn't offer him much of a deal.

However, if Janna kept the character door closed,

his past record wouldn't come in, not unless they could show a strong connection to his present charge.

But none of that mattered if the State was seeking to have him declared a Sexually Dangerous Person. All of this would come out. It all went to his propensity toward sexual crimes.

Janna chuckled to herself in disbelief. She hadn't been prepared for this surprise. She hadn't been prepared to argue her client was not a sexually dangerous predator. This changed things entirely, his case, his status in court, her chance to bargain on his behalf.

Damn him, she thought.

It wasn't surprising he had lied to her, wanting to leave his past buried. He would rather have her surprised in court and made to look completely foolish than risk having her think he was a pervert, and thus lose faith in his innocence. This was the story of 95% of the defendants she'd come across, on either side of the table.

He was right about one thing. Her belief in his innocence was long gone, but that didn't mean he wasn't entitled to representation. She had agreed to take him on. She was stuck with him. Although if he didn't start being honest with her, they would be slaughtered in court.

Chapter Fifty-five

680 North Lake Shore Drive
November 16
11:52 A.M.

Jordan Nash left Dr. Underwood's office feeling con-
flicted. She had remembered part of the license plate
number during her hypnosis session. It began with the
letters HZ. The problem was, she recalled the plates
during hypnosis and not afterward, as with her other
memories of the event. Detective Reilly said he
couldn't use her testimony or eyewitness account if she
continued to work with the hypnotherapist. But Dr.
Underwood was the only one helping her work
through the experience. He was helping her get past
that horrible night.

Jordan decided she would tell Detective Reilly she

wasn't seeing Underwood anymore and that she had remembered the license plate number on her own. The detective wasn't going to call the therapist. What did he care how she remembered, as long as they caught the guy?

She sighed, thinking her plan might not work. She was annoyed by the whole thing. She pushed the call button for the elevator a second time. What was taking so long? She leaned up against a marble wall and felt the cold seep through her silk sweater. She was tired, worn out from the trauma.

The bell finally rang, an elevator had arrived. Jordan rode it down several floors before reaching the lobby. She put her coat on and zipped it, pushing her hair back from her face so she could pull her tan chenille hat on. She walked towards the Erie Street exit.

That was when she saw him.

She froze on the spot. Her feet turned into lead blocks and she was unable to move. Her heart skipped a beat and started to race. A feeling of sheer panic hit her like a concrete truck, but she still couldn't move from the place she had stopped. Her eyes darted around the lobby, looking for another exit.

There was one going out to Lake Shore Drive, and another one going out to Huron Street. She was experiencing hot flashes, and waves of nausea washed over her. She realized she needed to use the restroom badly.

Jordan wanted to scream. She wanted to run as fast as she could, but her body wasn't responding. It was like waking up in the backseat of the car all over again.

A single tear rolled down her cheek, silently, as people brushed past her in the crowded lobby. Then she felt him, touching her arm. She closed her eyes.

When she opened them, he was gone. He had slipped past without recognizing her.

She opened her mouth and gulped in the warm lobby air, unaware until now she had been holding her breath. She began to cough loudly.

It was him. The detective from the Ram's Head Tavern. He had nudged her arm. He had actually touched her.

Jordan lifted her foot, which felt like a lead weight being dragged through water. It was like she was walking on the moon. She needed to call Detective Reilly. She pulled her cell phone out of her purse and checked the battery signal. There was one bar left. It was about to run out of power.

She walked outside and stopped on the sidewalk, shocked that she had seen the man who kidnapped her. Her phone had a signal. Still in disbelief, she dialed Detective Reilly's number from memory. There was no answer.

"Come on, damn it."

She felt a stream of hot, wet tears flooding her cheeks. She had been unaware she was crying. She wiped the tears away with the back of her hand.

Finally, Detective Reilly's voice mail picked up. She

got his emergency number and dialed, leaving him a message.

"Detective Reilly? It's Jordan Nash," she sputtered into the phone. "I'm here at my doctor's office. I'm outside the building. I had to leave. I . . . I just saw him, the man who attacked me. He's here, in the building. I know it was him, one hundred percent for sure. I don't know what to do right now. I'm at 680 North Lake Shore, but I can't stay here. I'm too scared."

Her phone beeped. "Hello?" she said into the receiver. She looked down at the phone. The battery had died.

"Damn it!" she shouted, throwing the phone back into her purse. She looked back at the building once more and then ran across the street.

Chapter Fifty-six

1149 West Adams Street
The Cop's Corner
November 16
12:37 P.M.

Reilly had visited the Ram's Head Tavern for a second time, to talk with the bartender who was working the night Jordan Nash was grabbed. He hadn't remembered much when Reilly first spoke with him. He remembered Jordan had been drunk and that she left with some strange guy, willingly. Not particularly helpful. Maybe the composite sketch would jog his memory.

Reilly showed Sal the sketch Jordan had come up with just for kicks, not expecting much.

"Nah, sorry, still nothing," Sal mumbled and turned

his back on Reilly. He didn't recognize the man in the sketch. It was a dead end.

Reilly frowned. Maybe the sketch was too rough. Either way, he didn't have anything to work with, so he went with his gut. Jordan thought the guy was a detective, so he needed to go where the police were. He figured he would try the cop shops, the equipment suppliers. It was worth a shot. If this guy really was a detective, someone might recognize him at one of the officer supply shops.

Usually owned by retired police officers, the supply shops were privately run businesses that sold everything from uniforms, leather jackets, flashlights and even gray wool blankets. Officers got an annual allowance for equipment and could spend it at whichever store they preferred and on whatever they needed. Most of the officers, including the detectives, shopped at The Cop's Corner downtown.

Reilly noticed a message waiting on his pager. He checked the time, almost half an hour ago. That was funny, he hadn't heard it go off. It could wait another minute. Catching this killer was his priority. He pushed open the door of the supply store and walked right over to the front counter, flashing his badge.

"Detective Sam Reilly, Area Two Violent Crimes," he said to the man at the counter.

"What can we do for you?" the older man asked.

"I'm investigating the kidnapping of a young woman who was dumped off on the South Side. We think the guy who grabbed her might be CPD, either that or pretending to be CPD."

The man behind the counter put his crossword down and looked over his glasses, straightening up on his stool.

"No kidding?"

"No kidding. You recognize this guy at all?" Reilly pulled the composite sketch from his pocket and unfolded it on the counter.

The man glanced down at the sketch for just a brief moment and his face started to turn white.

"That's him? The killer?" he asked.

"I don't know. It could be. Do you recognize him?"

"That's Hunter. Hunter's his last name. His first name is something like . . . gosh, I'm not sure. He comes in pretty regular, though."

"Yeah?" Reilly hadn't expected the man to recognize the face in the sketch. After all, Jordan hadn't even been sure. He was surprised, and a little doubtful.

"Are you sure? Take another look. Be very sure."

"I'm sure," the counterman replied, looking again at the sketch.

"He's a cop?"

"Used to be. I think he was at the Academy, he got thrown out or quit or something. I don't know. He said his dad was a cop and he just collects this stuff now."

"What's your name?" Reilly asked.

"Ray. Ray Keller."

"All right, Ray. Do you talk to this guy when he comes in?"

"I have before, yeah."

"How often does he come in? What's 'regular' mean?"

"Once a month. Maybe less. He stops in to look for gadgets, that sort of thing."

"He ever buy any blankets that you remember, by chance?"

"Sure, probably. He's bought a bunch of stuff from us."

"He ever shown you a badge?"

"No, nothin' like that. He don't buy badge-required supplies, just general stuff."

"When was the last time he came in?"

"A couple weeks ago maybe."

"You have any old receipts for him, credit card receipts?"

"Nope. He always pays in cash. He buys mostly little stuff, like I said. No real big-ticket items."

"Anyone else working here today?"

"Not until this afternoon. George will be in then."

"Okay," Reilly looked around the store. "You ever hear him say where he lives?"

"No, nothing like that. He don't say much. Said his dad was a police officer and that he was shot while on duty. He said he used to want to be a police officer, but he changed his mind after that. I don't know. He just comes in, picks a few things out, pays in cash and leaves. It's not real conversational."

"Thanks. You've been a big help. Call me if you remember anything else. And please have anyone else who works here that has any information about this man call me ASAP, okay?"

"I'll do that." Ray took Reilly's card.

Reilly left the supply shop quickly. He needed to run background for a possible Hunter, and call personnel to find out if they had any records for a Hunter.

Chapter Fifty-seven

Dr. Von Patton had run out of ideas for the moment. He hadn't been able to get into Dr. Shore's office. She left to use the restroom, as usual, but her door was locked. He tried to force it open but to no avail. His luck, and his patience, seemed to have expired.

He was sitting in a café around the corner from Dr. Shore's building, sipping a latte. He slammed two Xanax and a Tegretol to stop his hands from trembling. The drugs had stopped working weeks ago, but they were his last defense, his only shield from the demons that kept attacking his mind.

Why was God punishing him in this way? What had

he done to deserve this? He had tried so hard, but the pieces would not fall into place. These women, it was all their fault.

His attorney had betrayed him. He knew she would turn his records over to the State during the discovery process. He wasn't stupid. She couldn't be trusted. And neither could Dr. Shore. She would release his records just as soon as she was given a good enough reason.

All these women—what disappointments. He felt completely alone, utterly betrayed and cornered, with no way out. He knew he was going down. These women would see to his ultimate demise. Dr. Von Patton was desperate. Beyond desperate.

There was only one choice left for him, one final card for him to play. He wouldn't go out without leaving behind his legacy, no matter what the cost.

He picked up his latte, sipping slowly from the cardboard cup. His hands had stopped shaking, his body felt solid again, if only temporarily. He was prepared to work. With no one behind him, betrayed by everyone and everything, he needed to look ahead to the future. He had promised he would leave his mark on this world.

He wiped his mouth on the paper napkin and stood up from the small bistro table, where he had been seated.

The world hadn't heard the last of him yet. Not by a long shot.

Chapter Fifty-eight

Detective Reilly listened to Jordan's message for a second time, then called for backup. He floored the Chevy and pulled the car onto Columbus Drive. He wanted to get to her doctor's building as quickly as possible, in case the suspect was still there.

The streets were full with workers on their lunch breaks, people making their way back to the office. Reilly was losing time by dealing with the crowds. The blaring siren and light stuck to his roof wasn't clearing traffic fast enough for him.

Reilly heard his pager go off. He checked the number. It was the station. He called in on his cell phone.

"Yeah, Detective Reilly here. I just got paged."

"Reilly? It's Carol. We just got an emergency call from your kidnapping victim, Jordan Nash. She says she saw the suspect about an hour ago, in the 680 North Lake Shore building."

"I got the message. I'm on my way there. Dispatch sent backup. What else did the girl say?"

"She says he's the one who had her for sure. Says you have a composite sketch. She said his nose was a little different than she remembered, but that it was him."

Reilly pulled the sketch from his pocket and looked at the suspect's face again. "I've got you, you bastard," he said to the piece of paper.

Reilly asked Carol to contact Detective Stone, over at Area Four. He shouldn't have doubted Stone to begin with, but the guy seemed to be jerking Reilly around.

Reilly had withheld the forensics information from Stone. The gray wool blanket and blue wool fiber match up had thrown him through a loop. He didn't know whom he could trust, and with Stone acting so weird about sending over the autopsy reports on the Pilsen victims . . . well, he hadn't liked his stalling.

They were too close now. Ray Keller said the man in the sketch was not a police officer. It wasn't someone from the department, which although a relief, left a whole city full of suspects. He needed Stone's help, especially since Jordan's credibility crumbled with each visit to her doctor.

"Anything else?" Carol asked, snapping Reilly out of his zone.

"Yeah, can you run a search for me on the name Hunter?"

"You got a first name?"

"No, sorry, that's all I have."

"I'll see what I can do with just Hunter then. I'll do it now. You want arrests and outstanding warrants?"

"Please."

"Thanks, Carol."

"Oh, Reilly? One more thing."

"Yeah?"

"The victim, she says she remembered the first two letters of the license plate of the car she was in."

"Uh-huh. What'd she say?" Reilly asked, maneuvering in and out of traffic lines.

"H and Z. The first two letters of the plates are H, then Z. Henry, Zebra. Got it?"

"Gotcha. Thanks again."

Reilly hung up the phone. "Not a copper after all. Not with HZ plates." All police vehicles used an M, for municipal, as the first letter on the plate, even the undercover cars. This guy was obviously impersonating a police officer, right down to the car.

Reilly pulled his own car up to the front of the large 680 building. He looked up at the tall stone building, looming high over his head, casting its shadow down across Lake Shore Drive. There had to be hundreds of offices inside, he thought.

Two squad cars pulled up right after him, sirens blaring. The officers stepped out of their cars.

"Shit," Reilly cursed loudly.

"What's up?" one of the officers asked.

People were entering the building in flocks, finished with their noon break. "680 North Lake Shore, the Playboy building. I forgot. This place is huge. I don't know how we're gonna find the guy in here."

"Dispatcher said the Cross-Town Killer suspect was over here," the same officer asked.

"He was. But I don't know if he is now."

Reilly pulled out Jordan's sketch of the suspect. "Let's go in there and start looking for this guy." He handed the officers a copy of the sketch. "Start looking—and ask anyone you see if they've seen this guy. I'll make some more copies of the sketch."

Reilly bolted up the steps of the office building and walked into the lobby. He needed to get to the first office with a working copy machine. They were going to flood the building with this sketch.

Chapter Fifty-nine

680 North Lake Shore
November 16
4:12 P.M.

Lorna Shore stared at the composite the officer handed her before she went into session. She couldn't ignore the similarities. The resemblance was too close to shrug off as mere coincidence. She picked up the sketch from her desk and looked long and hard at the drawing one last time, before digging through her desk drawer for the business card.

Although the nose on the man in the sketch was a little off, she recognized his face immediately. The person in the drawing was Dr. Mason Von Patton. She was almost sure of it.

A caption under the sketch said to consider the man extremely dangerous. He was wanted for murder and kidnapping.

Lorna Shore blinked several times, her eyes assaulted by the dust that flew out of her bottom desk drawer.

Where was that damn card?

She had thrown it into the bottom drawer, not intending to ever use it. At the time she didn't even know why she was keeping it, but she was glad she had held on to it.

She really hadn't thought Von Patton capable of physically harming anyone. He was aggressive at times, but he always seemed under control during their sessions. There had to be some mistake.

Then why are you looking so hard for this business card?

The officer said the man in the sketch had been in the building that very afternoon. Was Von Patton in her building that day? The building was huge, filled with stores, doctor's offices, residences and more. It could have been anyone that was seen in the lobby area. There were always plenty of people coming in and out.

Her mind wouldn't let her off that easy, though. The man in the sketch looked too much like Von Patton. He could easily have been in the building that day. Could it really have been him? Perhaps even visiting another doctor, a colleague?

One thing was certain, the doctor hadn't been in to see her that day. In fact, he hadn't scheduled a session in weeks. He had cancelled his regular appointment and hadn't been back since.

Had he run out of medication? She prescribed refills for him, and besides, he could always write his own script if he needed it.

It couldn't be him. It had to be a coincidence, but her stomach was telling her otherwise.

Damnit, where was that card?

She pulled out a stack of business receipts from the drawer and the card fell to the carpet.

"Janna Scott, that's her name." Lorna Shore sighed with relief.

She didn't know why, but she couldn't bring herself to call the police. Not yet. She wasn't even sure the man in the sketch was Von Patton. She wasn't comfortable breaking the doctor-patient privilege, not until she was sure, sure that her patient had been the one who committed these crimes.

She dialed the number on Janna's business card, but the lawyer didn't pick up. Lorna got her voice mail. She hung up the phone.

What was she going to say anyway?

Maybe my patient is a murderer after all? Maybe his fantasies were more dangerous than I realized?

She rested her forehead in the palm of her hands. Lorna Shore, M.D., full of knowledge on people's motives for action, was unsure what action she herself should take. She was genuinely stumped.

Where was Dr. Von Patton? Why hadn't he been in to see her recently?

Damn you, Mason Von Patton for putting me in this position.

Lorna Shore reached for the phone again. She had no choice. She dialed Janna's number and, this time, left her a message.

Book VII

The Legacy

Chapter Sixty

Metzenstein Rare Coin and Stamp Dealers
212 North Clark Street
November 16
5:22 P.M.

Norie left the store a few minutes before her scheduled time. She was tired. She was eight months' pregnant and feeling every day of it. Her large stomach protruded from under even her bulky winter coat. Her face looked as if it were glowing. Her skin looked pure and milky white.

Dr. Von Patton watched her as she turned her head up toward the sky and shuddered, wrapping her coat tightly around herself. The weather had turned, almost overnight, as it always did in Chicago, and it had brought snow flurries to the Windy City. Snowflakes danced in the air, but refused to stick to the sidewalk when they landed.

It was perfect, absolutely perfect. Dr. Von Patton enjoyed the scene momentarily before pulling his Mercedes alongside the sidewalk where Norie was walking.

He rolled down the driver's side window of the car and leaned out.

"Norie? Norie Gallagher?"

She stopped walking and pulled the scarf away from her face to see who was talking to her.

"It's Dr. Von Patton, from the other day. I was just in your store, remember?"

"Oh, yes." Norie smiled, flashing a full set of pearly white teeth at him. "How are you?"

"Fine, thank you. You look too cold and uncomfortable to be walking very far."

"I'm not going far. Just around the corner, to the bus stop."

"The bus?" Dr. Von Patton shook his head. "In your condition? In the snow? Why don't you let me give you a ride?" he offered.

Norie stopped and tilted her head, thinking about accepting.

"Come on. Where are you headed?"

"I was planning to stop by my mom's house, if you're headed home?"

"I certainly am. Climb on in."

Dr. Von Patton leaned across the passenger seat and opened the Mercedes door for her. "I'm glad I can give you a lift," he said, as Norie heaved herself into the car.

"I appreciate it greatly. My husband was planning on picking me up today, but he was held up at the office."

"Good thing I'm here then."

Norie made herself comfortable in the car seat, as comfortable as possible, given her size.

Dr. Von Patton looked over at her and her large stomach. She seemed almost angelic beside him, like she knew her purpose.

"How far along are you?" he asked politely, fully aware of the answer.

"Eight months. I'm due just before Christmas." Norie beamed, obviously excited about the impending birth of her first child.

Dr. Von Patton pulled the car to the side of the road once they crossed over Congress Street.

"What would you think about moving that due date up by a few weeks?" he snarled.

"What? What are you talking about? Why are we stopping?" Norie looked confused, like a deer frozen before a car's headlights. The doctor knew she could sense what was to come. She tried the door handle but the door was locked. She lashed out at him.

Dr. Von Patton reached over and covered her mouth with a rag, holding her head with his arm, muffling her screams. He reached into his jacket pocket and pulled out a syringe. He quickly stuck her in the neck, injecting 50cc's of sodium pentathal into her jugular vein.

"Good night, sweet angel," he whispered in her ear.

Her eyes, once wide with fright, began to droop instantly after he administered the shot.

"You are assured a place in heaven. That, my dear, I promise you."

He pushed Norie's body over, her head thumping against the window. He turned the car around and drove toward the lab. He didn't have much time.

Chapter Sixty-one

Cook County Hospital
November 16
5:36 P.M.

"Nurse," James groaned.

"Nurse!" His throat was dry and his lips parched, making his voice barely audible. He blinked his eyes, looking around the curtained area he was lying in. He was in the hospital, but he couldn't remember how he had gotten there.

He reached down and pressed the call button. Through the curtains he saw the sky blue jacket of an attending physician, a woman. A sharp pain shot through the left side of his head, and he winced. The doctor was talking just outside his room, or curtain.

"If this doctor was treating him over at Clayton, we need to find out what for. He's not HIV positive. He's been tested here," James heard the woman doctor say.

"Well, he called here looking for James Johannis, the one we have," a second woman's voice answered.

James began to cough loudly. A nurse poked her head in, the same one he had just heard talking outside his curtained area.

"Oh my goodness!" the large black nurse exclaimed. "You're awake!"

James caught another glimpse of the doctor who had just been talking, and he started to remember.

"Could I have some water, please?" he asked the nurse.

"Of course. I'm Sarah, the main nurse for this section, at least for the time being."

"Who's the doctor?"

"Dr. Bloom? She's been visiting regularly to see how you've been coming along."

James winced again.

"Are you okay? Tell me what hurts," Sarah suggested.

"My head."

"I can give you some aspirin for it, but that's all for now. Let me get you that water. I'll send the doctor in to talk to you."

"No! No doctors," James begged in his strained and raspy voice.

"No doctors? Why? They're the ones who have been helping you."

James eyes grew wide with fright and he told her

again, "Do not bring a doctor in here. I'm fine. Just bring me some water."

"I'll be right back." Sarah rolled her eyes and mumbled to herself about how silly he was acting, then she disappeared out into the hallway.

She came right back, carrying a paper cup filled with water and two aspirin.

"Sip slowly at first. Your body isn't use to drinking so much right now," she advised him.

James did as he was told, sipping from the paper cup, allowing the water to seep into the crevices of his cracked lips and tongue, rehydrating his mouth.

Sarah watched him cautiously.

"Do you know your name?" she asked.

"What do you think I am? Some brain-dead reject?" James retorted sharply. "My name is James Johannis. I'm from Jamaica."

"Okay, good. Do you know how you got here?"

"Not exactly," he confessed. "How?"

"You were hit by a car. You jumped out a window, remember?"

James's memory began to perk up with Sarah's hints. "Damn straight I did, girl," he said.

"Didn't want to go back to jail?" Sarah guessed.

"Nah, it wasn't that at all. I remember a little bit."

James drank the rest of his water, and paused for a moment, collecting his thoughts and preparing his tongue to speak.

"I'm going to tell you something, and it stays between you and me for now, got it?"

"I got it."

"You're the one who's been watching my back while I've been laid up, right?"

"I ain't seen much of your back, honey," Sarah chuckled, amused that James's sassy personality seemed to have made a recovery.

"Ya know what I mean." His accent was thicker than usual. His own voice seemed foreign to him as he began to talk.

"There's a doctor, over at the jail. He got it in for me. That's why I jumped out the window, girl."

"Oh yeah? Why's that?" Sarah asked, clearly not believing him.

"I'm not joking now, you hear me out on this. There's a crazy, whacked-out doctor working over at the jail. He had it in for me 'cuz I know what he was up to. I heard him talking 'bout it."

"Talking about what?" Sarah couldn't resist the bait.

"He's injecting inmates with the AIDS virus, with HIV. I swear it to you. It's some mutation of the HIV virus, or somethin' like that. And he's not treatin' all of 'em either. I swear it to you."

"You're crazy. You need to go back to sleep, honey."

"I swear it, you have to believe me. I don't know how he hasn't found me already."

"You just woke from a coma, honey. It's all just a bad dream." Sarah tried to calm James down. "You're suffering from delusions obviously, so much talk about boogie men and demons."

"What?"

"The boogie man or whomever. You were always talking about him."

"Not boogie man, the boog man, that's what everyone called him," James said in his thick Jamaican accent. "He works with boogs as he says, you know, boogs and droogs, he call it."

"Oh! I get it!" Sarah finally understood. "The bug man! Bugs and drugs. Not the boogie man, the bug man you call him!"

"Yeah, the boog man," James repeated, wondering what she thought he was saying.

"Either way, there ain't no doctors injecting anyone with anything around here."

"Oh yeah? What makes you so sure? I'm tellin' you, girl, I heard him talking and saw his papers. He caught me looking at his stuff. I got word that he was comin' for me, jailhouse security, ya know." James snickered.

Sarah folded her arms, unconvinced by his story.

"That's why the numbers keep growing, at the jail. Don't you get it? That's why we got so many sick inmates." He shook his head, frustrated with Sarah.

"So why'd you jump out the window?"

"I got word he was coming for me next. He knew I was on to him."

"And he was that worried about this story of yours, worried that some inmate was going to report him, huh?"

"That's just it, it's not no story. He was 'fraid they would check him out if I told what I knew."

"Uh huh." Sarah rolled her eyes and shook her finger at him.

"You better watch who you go around, talking this way and all."

"That's why I'm saying, don't you go tellin' no one what I said and don't tell no one I'm here."

"They know you're here, honey. And no one's come for you yet," she said.

It was James's turn to disbelieve her. "You sure?"

"I'm positive. I haven't had to fight any doctors off, at least not in the last few days." She grinned. "What'd you say this doctor's name was?"

James thought for a second, closing his eyes tightly.

"Dr. Mason Von Patton. He works over at Twenty-sixth and California. Works with the HIV and the AIDS patients.

"Dr. Von Patton, that's your doctor, the one who called here earlier for you."

"He ain't my doctor. I'm no AIDS patient."

"I know, I saw your chart. Wondered why he was looking for you."

"That's what I'm telling you. He's looking for me because he knows I seen him. He knows I know what he's been doin', poisoning inmates."

"That sounds awfully evil. Are you sure you know what you heard?" Sarah squinted her eyes.

"I swear to you, I swear it. You can't let him in here to see me."

"He's not coming here. I told him that your chart showed you weren't HIV positive. Anyway, I told him that it would be silly for him to come 'specially over to see you when we have plenty of Infectious Disease doctors right here."

"What did he say?"

"He said he thought he should see you himself."

"I told him, 'Why don't you just tell me what he's on, what you've been giving him and I'll have one of our ID docs look at him?' and then he hung up on me."

"See, I'm tellin' you, he's out to get me. He knows I know, about the monster inside him. Sarah, you've gotta believe me."

"It is odd he wanted to come over to see you. Well, why don't you just get a good night's rest and we'll look into it tomorrow. I promise. He's not going to come for you tonight."

"Tomorrow might be too late."

"Tomorrow's the best I can do. I'm off for the rest of the night. First thing in the morning. I'll check it out," she promised.

Sarah turned and left James alone in his room.

Chapter Sixty-two

Cook County Hospital
November 16
6:11 P.M.

Essie was getting ready to go home for the night and
see her daughter when Sarah walked into the staff
locker area.

"Hi, Sarah," Essie said, cheerfully.

"Hey, Essie. How've you been, dear? I haven't seen
you for a while."

"I can't complain. Where do they have you working
these days?"

"I'm assigned to the jail section still. Gail's out on
maternity leave. I'm filling in until she gets back."

"How's that going?"

Sarah took her coat from her locker and started to

put it on. She sighed and bowed her head a little, then laughed. "You don't want to know, trust me."

"Why do you say that? What's going on?"

"Nothing. It's just these inmates—they're a handful. I had one come out of a six-week coma today. I think they kept his brain there, wherever he was for the past six weeks, if you know what I mean."

"I do. Sometimes I get the same type of behavior from the ID patients, especially the really sick ones."

"Well, this guy is one of those paranoid types. He thinks our staff is out to get him. Doesn't want to see any doctors."

"Aren't they all like that? No one likes their doctor here, I swear."

"This guy thinks the doctors actually are out to get him though, thinks one wants to kill him. Claims the doctor was injecting inmates with HIV and he found out about it. What a loon, huh?"

Essie rolled her eyes, "Oh, señora! You do have your hands full! I pity you."

"I know. He wants me to look into this doctor for him or something like that. Like I'm supposed to play *Charlie's Angels* for him."

Essie laughed as her friend imitated an angel, shooting and chopping at the air.

"Who's the doc?" she asked.

"Some Von Patton. I don't know him."

Essie stopped giggling and stared her friend straight in the face. "Dr. Mason Von Patton?"

"Yeah, that's what he said." Sarah remembered, once Essie said his full name.

"He's one of my doctors," she told Sarah.

"Really? You seen him running around with any needles lately?" Sarah was still laughing.

Essie wasn't. "What's this patient of yours saying?" she asked curiously.

Sarah briefly recounted James's version of the events taking place at the jail and Clayton Health Services, the medical facility that served the Cook County Jail inmates.

Essie was concerned and the change in her demeanor wasn't lost on Sarah.

"What's wrong, Ess? Why are you getting all serious on me?"

"It's just that, well . . ." Essie hesitated, but decided to go on. "Dr. Von Patton's name keeps popping up all over, and he's always in some kind of trouble. I had an attorney calling me the other day, asking me questions about him."

"And?"

"I don't know." Essie picked up her bag, preparing to leave the staff room.

"Essie, come on. You really think this nut is telling the truth? A delusional post-comatose inmate? You really think this Dr. Von Patton is injecting patients with tainted blood and then not treating them?"

Essie's mind was in overdrive. She closed her eyes, wanting to believe Sarah was right. She kept thinking about all the files in his office, all the sick patients of his who didn't get better, and the attorney calling.

"It's like the Tuskegee story," Essie whispered.

"What? You're going crazy now too, girl."

"Think about it, Sarah. Where the doctors didn't treat all those men who were dying of syphilis—just let their bodies rot out. Happened right here in America, down in Macon County, Alabama."

"Oh stop it. This is the year 2000 and we're not in the deep South, we're in the middle of Chicago, a huge city," Sarah replied.

Essie noticed Sarah seemed a bit shaken for all her naysaying.

"I have a bad feeling about Dr. Von Patton, Sarah."

"So what do you want to do about it?"

"I want to talk to your patient, your inmate."

"All right, if you really want to."

Essie called her mom, who agreed to watch Mariah, and then she went to talk to James, who after some cajoling from Sarah, retold his tale of misfortune.

After hearing his story, Essie was dumbfounded. She didn't know whom to believe or what to think. So she took the only next logical step. She placed a call to Janna Scott.

Chapter Sixty-three

Stone finally tracked down his missing partner. Arnie
had been holed up in Wisconsin. He had rented a lake
cabin and had been getting drunk for the past week.
Internal Affairs was fuming mad they hadn't been able
to talk to him. Then, out of the blue, he called Stone
in the middle of the night, and in the middle of a serial murder investigation.

Stone hadn't slept a wink afterward. He still wanted
to help Arnie, but he wouldn't destroy police reports.
Even though he hated to ask, Stone had questioned
Arnie about the missing Pilsen victim reports. As it
turned out, they had been misplaced in Arnie's files all

along. Stone made copies of the reports and, after getting a frantic call from Area Two, he left to meet Detective Reilly at Chicago's Playboy building.

He arrived just as Reilly and his backup were finishing canvassing the building. He and Reilly were talking in the building's lobby.

"What the hell happened here anyway?" he asked Reilly when things finally settled down in the lobby.

"Our kidnapping victim, Miss Jordan Nash, was here this afternoon and saw him, saw the killer."

"She's gone?" Stone asked.

"Yeah, she took off right away. She called to let us know, then boom . . . she disappears. I had this composite she'd been working on with the sketch artist, and we just started canvassing the building."

"Where's she at now, do we know?"

"I don't know. No one's been able to locate her."

"Do you think he has her?"

"It's tough to say. No one in the building has recognized him from the sketch. So no one can place him with Ms. Nash."

"What else do you have?"

"Nothing. What do you have?" Reilly shot back, still feeling a touch competitive with Stone.

"I brought the autopsy reports and the fiber analysis for the Pilsen women."

Reilly took the reports and flipped through them briefly, stopping at the fiber analysis reports.

"Just what I thought," he mumbled to himself.

"What did you think?" Stone asked, puzzled.

"Blue and gray fibers. On the Pilsen victims. I sent control samples from a 1999 Chevy Caprice and a standard-issue police blanket into the crime lab."

"Yeah?" Stone thought he knew where Reilly was going with this, but couldn't believe it.

"It was a match. The dyes were from different batches, but the fibers were the same."

"No shit. So the guy's a cop then?"

"Well, I thought so, and I went over to The Cop's Corner. They recognized the sketch. Said the guy comes in and buys equipment often. Calls himself Hunter. And as it turns out, the guy's probably not a copper. The counterman said he might have been an Academy dropout or something. Just posing as an officer. Probably drives a Chevy Caprice."

"And this is him?" Stone asked, looking down at the sketch drawing in his hand.

"Yup. And the first two letters of his plates are HZ."
Stone's head jerked up. "For sure?"

"That's what Miss Nash says."

"Then what are we wasting our time here for? Let's get a DMV check on these plates."

"I hear you."

The two men left the building and had dispatch put in a request to have the plates run. A short while later, they came up with three potential addresses to which the plates were registered.

"None are registered to anyone named Hunter."

"Probably using an alias," Stone guessed.

"Probably."

"You want to take two and I'll take one?" Stone offered. "Or you want to go together?"

"We can split to save time. Our guy probably knows he was spotted here today. He may be getting ready to flee. He may even have Jordan Nash, I don't know."

"All right. I'll take the Indiana address."

"Agreed." Reilly started to walk away, then suddenly turned back. "Oh, Stone?"

"Yeah?"

"One more thing."

"Uh huh?"

"Autopsy reports came back on the hair stylist, from Beaubien Woods."

"What'd we get out of that?"

"You know they found Scotch tape under the victim's fingernails at the scene, right?"

"I didn't know that."

"It doesn't matter, because it wasn't tape after all."

"What was it?"

"A stamp hinge. For adhering stamps to a collector's book."

Stone looked at Reilly, confused.

"Don't ask me—I'm just telling you what the report said."

"Thanks," Stone said, and the two detectives parted ways.

Chapter Sixty-four

Janna got Lorna Shore's message before she left the office. It seemed Dr. Shore's loyalty to her patient was rapidly dissipating. Shore said the police had been distributing flyers in her building. On the flyers was a sketch of a man wanted for kidnapping and murder. The man looked just like Doctor Von Patton. The flyer hinted the man was the Cross-Town Killer.

Lorna Shore's voice trembled on the recorder. She was scared. She asked if Janna thought Von Patton was responsible for the killings that had been in the papers.

Janna hadn't returned Shore's call, because the next thing she knew, her phone was ringing again. This time it was Essie Ruiz calling her, telling her she should get to the hospital right away. Essie had some important information about Von Patton, but she wasn't willing to talk on the phone.

Janna wondered what was going on. All Dr. Von Patton's supporters seemed to be caving. And to be perfectly honest, they weren't the only ones. Janna herself was questioning why she ever agreed to take his case. The man was clearly a repeat sex offender, and sex offenders were known for their pathological lying.

But instead of preparing a motion to withdraw from the case, she decided to meet Essie at Cook County Hospital. She doubted if she had enough reason to request a withdrawal from the court anyway. And on top of that, she had already used Von Patton's retainer to pay her last two months' rent.

Janna made it in no time to Cook County Hospital, where she met Essie at the hospital entrance. Essie escorted her to the hospital's jail section.

When Janna entered his room, James was sitting up watching television. He glanced at her when she came in, then returned to watching the evening news.

"James, this is the lady friend of mine I was telling you about, the attorney," Essie said.

"My name is Janna Scott. I'm a criminal defense attorney." Janna extended her hand to James.

"I don't want to see no attorneys neither. I've had it with lawyers and doctors both. So you might as well go on back to wherever it is you came from," James said in his thick accent.

"I can't do that, James. Essie is a witness for me in a case I'm working on and she says you have some important information for me about my client, Dr. Von Patton. I don't want to have to subpoena you, but if you want it that way . . ."

"He your client? You represent that fool?" James snorted in disbelief. "I ain't tellin' you nothing then."

"What if I told you I could help get you out of jail faster?" she asked.

James raised his eyebrows. "I'd say you and a hundred others have made that promise, lady."

"I mean it, though. I used to work for the State's Attorney. I have a lot of contacts there. I can help you."

"You can help me with my court case?"

"I can."

"Even if I want a trial?"

"Certainly. As long as there is no conflict of interest between your case and Dr. Von Patton's case."

"There ain't no conflicts, believe me. I was grabbed for stealing a toilet, doesn't have a thing to do with Von Patton. I don't know much 'bout your laws, but I don't see how there can be any conflict between my stealin' a toilet and what he's been doing."

"And what is it that he has been doing?"

324

James peered at her sideways and folded his arms. She sat in a chair next to his bed and put her bag on the floor. She wasn't leaving until this man told her what he knew about Dr. Von Patton. She had to know what she was working against.

"Can you tell me your story? The one you told Ms. Ruiz."

"I can," James finally agreed. He took a sip of water and Janna leaned in closer, eager to hear every word.

After James finished telling her about how Von Patton had been using the inmates as lab rats, Janna sat back in her chair without saying a word. She was thinking about whether she could afford to return a portion of Dr. Von Patton's retainer and keep the remaining portion, the portion she had used on rent, for her time spent thus far.

One thing was certain, her client was a complete whacko, and she wasn't up to handling his defense. She hated to admit it, but she believed James's story. She had seen plenty of lying defendants to be a good judge of when a person was telling the truth. She recognized a lie when she heard one, and James was not lying.

The worst part of it was she felt she couldn't give Von Patton a fair defense, not knowing what he was about.

She stood up from her chair and looked at Essie. She

was stunned, horrified, but tried not to let her face show it. She didn't know what to think. She had been a State's Attorney for crying out loud. Now this? This wasn't what she had in mind when she opened her own practice. She had to get herself off this case. She didn't want any part of this madness.

"Thank you for calling me, Essie. And thank you, James, for sharing this information with me."

"What are you going to do?"

"I'll be in touch with you. Soon, I promise." She picked her bag up from the floor and swung it over her shoulder.

Janna turned to leave the room, but stopped when she heard the news reporter's voice blaring out from the television set behind her.

"It is believed at this time that the mayor's daughter, Noreen Gallagher, has been kidnapped. She is eight months' pregnant. Eyewitness reports say she left the Metzenstein Rare Coin and Stamp Store, where she worked and got into a dark-colored Mercedes. She appeared to know the driver. Another witness reports seeing a struggle in the same car several blocks away from Metzenstein's Stamps. He called the police, but no one has been able to identify the driver. If you have any information regarding the vehicle or the whereabouts of Noreen Gallagher, please contact your local authorities immediately."

After hearing the report, Janna turned back over her shoulder and peered up at the television set. A picture of Noreen Gallagher was on the screen. A gold cross dangled from her neck.

Janna shuddered. She remembered Von Patton had been at Metzenstein's the other day. He also collected stamps and lived several blocks from the mayor. Could he have seen Noreen there? Coming and going? That is crazy, she told herself. Her client was not this sick.

It had to be coincidence. It was just too much of a leap. What was she going to do anyway? Call the police and tell them she was a criminal defense attorney and that she thought her client might have grabbed the mayor's daughter? Just turn her client in for a crime he may not even have committed, with no evidence?

Brilliant idea, Janna.

No. What she needed to do was to start thinking rationally. James's story had gotten to her, that was all. Coupled with the call from Lorna Shore, she was all worked up. Her mind was playing tricks on her.

Janna didn't say another word. She handed James her business card and told him she'd call him the next day.

"I'm counting on you. You better not let me down," he said.

She smiled grimly. "I won't."

She wrapped her coat around her shoulders and left Essie and James in the hospital room. She was freaking out, but they had no idea. She was going to Von Patton's house. She was getting off this case now. She wasn't going to let him scare her. She'd been confronted by some of the worst criminals the system had to offer, much worse than some weasel doctor. She was done with Dr. Von Patton.

Chapter Sixty-five

Janna walked around the exterior of the house, checking the doors to see if they were locked. They were. Von Patton hadn't answered the doorbell. She doubted if he was home. She tried to peer through the windows on the side of the house. She was peeking through a long, tall French-style window at what appeared to be the doctor's study.

She could see his desk, littered with papers. She noticed the legal captions on several papers, probably his court notices. From where she was crouched, she couldn't tell. The house was dark inside and the only way Janna could see anything at all was with the small flashlight she had brought from her glove compartment. Since Dr. Von Patton wasn't home, Janna decided to walk around the house and spy through his windows, trying to glimpse what she could with her little light.

She had no idea what she was looking for, or even what she had been thinking when she rushed over here to quit the case. But she was here now, and curiosity had gotten the better of her. She walked around the back of the house and saw a detached garage. There was a car parked in front of the garage. She never asked Von Patton what kind of car he drove, but the car parked outside the garage was a Chevy Caprice Classic. She sighed with relief that it wasn't a Mercedes, the car the news reporter said was used to kidnap Noreen Gallagher.

She had been allowing her mind to mess with her. She had been overreacting.

Maybe Von Patton wasn't half as bad as she had thought. She should go home, take a hot bath and forget about the whole thing—James, Lorna Shore, Kelsey Dore, all of it. She would talk to Von Patton first thing in the morning. However, instead of walking back to her own car, she approached the blue Chevy, very carefully. She chastised herself.

Come on, Janna, you're being ridiculous. Too much time spent over at 26th and California, that's what this is.

She walked up to the car and shined her flashlight through its windows. She could see some magazines on the front seat. She squinted, trying to see the titles.

She tried the door handle on the passenger side of the car. To her surprise, it had been left unlocked. She opened the door slowly, trying to be quiet.

What are you doing? You are snooping, trespassing on your own client's property. Whose side do you think you're on?

But Janna didn't stop, didn't close the car door. She bent over, leaned into the car's passenger area, and flipped through the papers on the car seat. She noticed some bills for lab space at City Memorial. She saw a Scott's catalog of stamps and a *Chicago Social* magazine.

Something told her to pick up the *Chicago Social* magazine. She did. A couple pages of the magazine were dog-eared. She opened the magazine, flipping to the marked page.

What she saw horrified her. There on the dog-eared pages were several photos of Noreen Gallagher and her husband. The caption read, *Eight months' pregnant and proud to be of public service.* Noreen Gallagher was smiling, holding her stomach. The article talked about the fund-raisers for Children's Memorial Hospital and other public interest groups she regularly helped.

Why was this page marked? Perhaps the doctor attended the fund-raiser. After all, he was a doctor. It was a fund-raiser for a hospital. But Janna knew better.

She closed the magazine and shut the car door. The stamp catalog, the picture of Noreen—could it really be true? What was she to do about it? She knew she couldn't call the police, not on her own client. And certainly not with a magazine and a stamp catalog as proof of his guilt.

Janna thought for a second. She had to do something. Could she call Jack Stone? Although they had been out, she didn't know him well enough to trust him with something like this. Or did she?

She opened the car door again and took down the address of Von Patton's lab space. She didn't know where else to look for him. And she knew she had to find him. The tightness in her chest wouldn't ease up until she did.

Chapter Sixty-six

1918 South Indiana
November 16
8:58 P.M.

Twenty minutes earlier, Detective Stone had seen the flicker of a flashlight as he walked to his car. He turned and crept away from it, listening to the person moving around the house.

He had waited quietly, lurking in the neighboring house's gangway. He crept through the yards of the other houses and watched. He gasped when he realized who it was.

It was Janna Scott. She was looking through his car.

Stone didn't make a sound, just waited until she had closed his car door and walked away. The cool evening air wasn't stopping the beads of sweat that kept dripping off his brow, hitting him on the chin. His face glistened and he was tired from crouching for so long. He grunted when he finally stood and emerged from the shadow of a large bush.

Damnit.

Why was Janna here? What was going on?

After leaving Reilly, he had gone to Von Patton's house, hoping to find him home. No one had answered the door.

Dr. Mason Von Patton was the registered owner of a 1998 Chevy Caprice Classic with license plates HZI4782. Since he didn't see the car in the driveway, Stone had decided to check out the surrounding areas of the house and garage.

By the back door he had found a pair of hiking boots covered in purple looseleaf.

Bingo.

He remembered the hair stylist's body had been dumped in a patch of purple looseleaf in Beaubien Woods. The plant was practically nonexistent in Illinois, except for in Beaubien Woods, where it flourished. Stone also had found the Chevy Caprice parked in the garage. The car was just like his own, except for the license plates.

That had given him his probable cause to enter the house. No one had heard from Jordan Nash yet and Stone believed Von Patton might have her in the house. He had gone in on his own, without a request for backup. He didn't have time to wait for help, not if Von Patton had the girl in there.

Stone had forced his way in through the back door. As it turned out, the house was empty. Stone had picked up some magazines and papers from a table near the rear door. He planned to take them to the crime lab for fingerprinting. He had put the magazines on his car seat, but when he saw the flashlight coming, he hid.

Now, Janna had just handled the entire stack of papers, which meant he would have to go back in for fingerprint samples.

But the real question was, what was Janna doing here?

He racked his brain to remember what she had told him about her current client list. She mentioned that she had a sex offender, a doctor. And he thought he remembered her saying that the guy was arrested over here and brought to Central Station. The name, Von Patton, it did sound familiar.

Was this her client's house?

If it was, why was she creeping around? What in the hell was she up to, he wondered? Did she know something? Was she protecting the guy?

Janna walked over to her own car. She was leaving. Stone quickly crept back to his car, started it, and pulled out into traffic, keeping Janna's car in sight. He radioed into dispatch. He was following her.

Chapter Sixty-seven

City Memorial Lab
November 16
9:13 P.M.

Dr. Von Patton heaved Norie up onto the lab table, exhausted from the strain of dragging her large and bloated body. The building was empty. Everyone had gone home for the night. He was alone in the lab with Norie.

He knelt on the ground and leaned forward on the table. He began to sob uncontrollably with his head bent down and buried in his arms. He was shaking. He looked out the window and noticed the moon, a glowing bulb of light set against the dark blue velvet sky. He knew he needed to be strong if he was to carry out his purpose this evening.

His mind flashed back to his childhood, to his mother and father. He could remember them arguing. His bedroom had been right next to his parents', and he had often overheard their fights. His mother had hated his father. Her hatred had carried over into the bedroom regularly, and she lashed out against his unwanted sexual advances. She had been filled with hatred for the man who had trapped her.

His father had raped his mother, date rape. And from their rage-filled encounter he had been conceived, spawned from his father's hate and his mother's fear. His father was a local police officer and no one would have believed his mother's story. In order to avoid bringing her small-town family shame, she had been forced to marry his father. And not a day of his lonely and shameful childhood went by that he hadn't thought about it, about who he was and why he was here. He had spent his childhood locked in a bedroom darkened by its blackened windows and bent over a tiny cot in prayer. While locked in that darkness he had seen the light, he had come to understand his purpose. He was here to correct the hatred that had brought him forth.

His body trembling and his mind spinning in every direction, Dr. Von Patton did not reach for his medication. Instead, he let himself evolve, transcend his physical self. He became the Soldier, a man so powerful, so free of fear, he stared death in the face and laughed. As the Soldier, Dr. Von Patton was comfortable, free of the nagging tension that drove him to find his next victim. Once he found her, he felt fulfilled, it was an indescribable release. He took several deep breaths and rose from the floor, where he had been kneeling before Norie.

He unbuttoned Noreen Gallagher's shirt, exposing her large, round stomach. Her skin was pulled taut and seemed almost luminescent in the dimmed lights of the lab. The Soldier began to pray for his child.

"Hail Mary, Mother of God, blessed is thy fruit of thy womb . . ." His voice trailed off. He repeated himself, chanting, "Blessed is thy womb, blessed is thy womb." He reached down into a duffel bag he had brought in earlier that day and pulled out a jar of iodine. He dabbed the iodine onto Norie's mound of a stomach and began to rub her lower belly, making large circles with his hands, watching the dark brown swirl across her skin.

The Soldier knew this was meant to be. It was intended for the child. If he was to leave this place, this city, and be forced into hiding, he needed to take a child with him. Someone he could love and teach and raise to do the work he would have to leave behind. And not just any child would do. No, his child would come from proper lineage, from political royalty.

The Soldier knew this was the only way he could leave his mark on the world. His legacy would live on through this child, the unborn child of Noreen Gallagher. His light would shine on through this golden child with a worthy political destiny, with a blessed lineage, unlike his own. It was through this political baby that he would infect the world with his message, that he would continue his work and spread his dream. He would purify the nation through politics—through the child. He would create a religion for the modern age and bring it into this world through his new child.

The Solider continued to rub Norie's stomach with the iodine and tried to determine the best place to make the incision.

Chapter Sixty-eight

City Memorial Hospital
November 16
9:40 P.M.

Janna didn't know why she had come to the lab. She was acting like a possessed, overzealous prosecutor, not a defense attorney. She wanted to confront him. At least, that's what she told herself. She wanted to call him on his lies, his manipulations, his antics. She wanted to pull the plug on it all. Janna wanted to quit, and tonight.

When she entered the small brick building that housed the lab, she noticed the security guard slumped in his chair. She crept slowly up to the man, thinking he had probably fallen asleep. She would just sneak past him. Why alert him to her presence?

Yes, why alert him to your trespassing? You can't go snooping through your client's lab if you wake up the guard.

Part of her did not want to go into the lab and discover whether James was telling the truth. A bigger part of her wanted to see the lab, though. Besides, she didn't think it too absurd that she might be looking for her client at his work. Even if it was later in the evening, he was a busy doctor. He could be at the lab.

At least that's how I'll explain it to the Attorney Discipline Commission when Von Patton reports my behavior.

As Janna neared the sleeping security guard, she thought his head looked kind of funny. It didn't seem like a very comfortable position for sleeping. She glanced back, but slipped quietly past the desk.

Maybe the security guard wasn't sleeping. Maybe his neck had been broken. His head was hanging there like a fallen scarecrow's. She took a couple of steps backward, trying to get a closer look.

You're going crazy. Just move on. Go.

The guard's neck did look broken, though. She was sure of it. She didn't want to get any closer.

Why would his neck be broken? He was sleeping, that was all.

Janna continued to move through the hallways of the quiet building, noticing the room numbers next to each door she passed.

She was looking for 203-B. It must be upstairs. She saw an elevator right in front of her and decided to take it up. She didn't want to get locked in some stairwell.

The elevator car was waiting on the first floor and

Janna got in and hit the button for floor two. The ride up was quick. She stepped off and looked both ways, guessing which way she should try first. She didn't have to wait long for an answer.

Down the hallway, she heard glass shattering. She pushed her hair back from her face and silently crept down the hallway, toward the noise. She could see light coming from underneath the fourth doorway on the right.

Chapter Sixty-nine

City Memorial Lab
November 16
9:43 P.M.

Janna stood with her back pressed against the wall right outside the lab. She could see the interior light spilling into the hallway from under the door. She could also hear someone banging around and she thought she heard a man's voice from behind the doorway. The noises were muffled. She thought about knocking on the door. He might not be able to hear her, though.

Who are you kidding? You want to catch him in the middle of something in there. At least be honest with yourself.

She mustered up all her courage and counted to

three. On three, she flung the door open while still standing pressed up against the wall. She poked her head through the doorway and looked inside the lab. She saw her client, Dr. Mason Von Patton, standing there dumbfounded, his mouth wide open.

"Dr. Von Patton? It's Janna Scott," she said, entering the lab.

The doctor, startled by the sudden intrusion, dropped something out of his hand. The low light in the lab glinted off the piece of metal as it fell to the floor with a clatter.

Janna couldn't believe her eyes as she took in the scene in the lab. A half-naked woman was lying upon a steel lab table, not moving. Her pregnant body seemed lifeless. Her stomach was almost offensive, covered in a reddish-brown oily substance, bubbling up from her otherwise tiny body.

What in the world was he doing in here?

Janna moved her eyes down the limp body of the woman on the table until she got to her face. She recognized the young woman from the *Chicago Social* magazine she had flipped through at his house. The young woman lying on the table was Noreen Gallagher, the mayor's daughter.

Briefly assessing the scenario, Janna tried to back up slowly, moving toward the door she had just come through.

"Leaving so soon, counselor? Why don't you stay for a while?"

"I came to talk to you about the hearing. I haven't

been able to get a hold of you anywhere and it's coming up in the next couple of days. I thought we needed to talk about your prior convictions and what our strategy would be," she lied.

Janna pled with Dr. Von Patton, "I don't know what's going on here, but I'm your attorney. I can help you. Let me go and get some help. We can work through this."

She attempted to calm him, to soothe him with the soft tones of her voice. He wasn't biting. The doctor moved from behind the table and started toward her.

She turned to run and was almost to the door when she felt his strong grasp on her shoulder, yanking her back, jerking her toward him.

She spun around and clobbered him in the jaw with her bag, its heavy contents striking his head with a loud thump.

The doctor reached up and felt his cheek, pausing momentarily to stare her squarely in the face. He started to laugh, a deep laugh that seemed to come straight from the depths of his dark soul.

"Counselor, that's quite a punch you pack there."

She furtively glanced sideways and realized she was too far away from the door to make it through without him grabbing her. She noticed a small microscope on the lab counter next to her.

"You don't want to do this, Dr. Von Patton. I'm the best thing you have going for you right now," she warned.

"If that's true, I don't want to know what my obstacles are going to be."

"Listen to me, Von Patton."

But he wasn't listening anymore. He lunged at her, trying to encircle her with his bearlike arms. She moved equally fast, picking the microscope up from the counter and swinging it sideways, crushing it into his skull.

He stumbled a few feet sideways and landed heavily on a second steel lab table, which was strewn with test tubes. The test tubes were knocked over and began to roll across the table before shattering on the tile floor.

Janna had been knocked to the ground when Von Patton lurched at her, and she felt a sharp pain in her tailbone.

"Brings whole new meaning to the phrase 'attorney-client relationship,' doesn't it, counselor?"

Janna moaned from the ground. She had fallen hard onto her backside. She tried to pick herself up, but Von Patton was right on top of her, kicking her back to the floor. She heard his sinister laugh coming from above her, and rolled over onto her side. He kicked the middle of her back, sending more pain radiating throughout her entire body.

Stand up, Janna. Just get up.

Suddenly, he moved away from her. Through blurred vision, she saw him over by Noreen. She managed to pull herself up from the floor and started to limp toward the door.

Broken vials and test tubes were lying all over the ground, and the blood that had spilled out from them was causing her to slide on the sticky tiles. She started hobbling towards the exit.

Von Patton was on her again though, knocking her down once more. She hit the floor, landing on her side this time, and went sliding through the brown oozy blood that was coating the lab aisle. Janna realized what was in the vials and started to panic.

The broken test tubes probably contained HIV-positive blood and the blood from the doctor's AIDS patients. This was Von Patton's AIDS research lab. She was lying in one big viral puddle. She still couldn't see well and her eyes were stinging, but she felt something cool and wet splashing up onto her arms. She could smell the pungent fumes saturating the dead air. It was gasoline. He must have brought it in with him earlier.

Dr. Von Patton planned to burn this lab down, and her along with it.

Chapter Seventy

City Memorial Lab
November 16
9:48 P.M.

Stone heard the commotion as soon as he got off the elevator. He had followed Janna all the way to the lab and realized she was probably headed to see her client, the very man Stone wanted to find. Planning to surprise Von Patton, he entered the building silently right behind Janna. When he stepped off the elevator, he heard a ruckus coming from the right. With his .44 drawn, he cautiously moved down the hallway.

Stone knew there was trouble inside. He had seen the broken neck of the security guard and realized he was walking into a time bomb. He couldn't turn back, though, not with Janna already inside. He had known

Janna for years and cared about her, and he had finally gotten the chance to date her. He had to make sure she was okay. He had to go in after her.

Sliding down the hallway wall, he approached the lab door. He caught a glimpse of the inside of the lab and saw a man, presumably Von Patton, moving around Janna, dousing the lab floor with gasoline. His back was to the door.

Stone saw his opportunity and he erupted through the doorway in a flash of energy. He tackled Von Patton from behind. He pushed him hard with his upper body, wanting to knock him away from Janna. With his gun still drawn, he yelled, "Police! Freeze, asshole!"

Von Patton stumbled forward a few paces and made a run for it.

Stone shot, firing off two rounds. Von Patton was too quick, though. He hadn't moved forward, but sideways. Stone's bullets hit the back wall of the lab.

Removing a lit Bunsen burner from a countertop, Von Patton smashed it onto the ground. A small fire started on the floor near him. The burning alcohol from the broken Bunsen burner was trailing toward the gasoline puddle Von Patton had left near the windows.

Stone looked over at Janna. She had pulled herself off the floor and was reaching for a fire extinguisher in the lab.

"What do you think, counselor? Think you can get me out of this mess? What's our defense going to be?" Dr. Von Patton was laughing, dragging his leg behind him.

Stone realized Von Patton had caught a bullet in the leg.

"I think I'm officially withdrawing from your case," Stone heard Janna yell.

The burning trail of alcohol hit the gasoline and a wall of flames sprung up, separating Von Patton and Norie from Stone and Janna.

"Just give it up, man!" Stone shouted across the flames. "You've got no way out!"

Norie was still lying motionless on the lab table as the flames began to ensconce her. Janna, watching as the flames crept closer, stood up and sprayed the room with the extinguisher, sending white foam flying everywhere.

"Damn it!" Stone yelled, having lost sight of Von Patton.

When he regained his sight, he saw Von Patton barreling through a fire exit at the rear of the lab. Stone rubbed his eyes and turned to Janna quickly.

"Are you okay?"

She nodded, unable to speak.

"Are you sure? I've got to go after him."

"Go. Please, go," Janna whispered.

"Can you check the girl?"

"I will."

Stone darted through the fire exit, right behind Dr. Von Patton.

Chapter Seventy-one

City Memorial Lab
November 16
9:53 P.M.

After Stone disappeared out the door, Janna looked over at Norie's body lying limp on the steel lab table. She noticed her large belly rising like a pitcher's mound from her otherwise small frame. Her stomach was stained with dark brown iodine circles. Janna hurried over to her side. She picked up her hanging arm and felt her wrist for a pulse. It was faint, but it was there.

She leaned over the girl's face and felt Norie's breath hot against her cheek. She was breathing. There was hope.

Janna checked her pregnant stomach. It was untouched with the exception of the iodine smears. There was no incision. Her baby was safely inside her womb. Janna knew there was a chance for her.

She looked around the room for her bag. She saw it on the floor near the door, among the shattered glass. Janna ran for her bag and pulled out her cell phone. She immediately dialed 911, but even as she did so she heard the sirens outside. It must be Stone's backup, she thought.

Janna pushed a strand of strawberry blond hair off her face and let out a huge sigh of relief for the first time. She knew help was near. Norie was going to make it. She went back to the woman's side and put her hand over her forehead. She saw Norie's eyelids flutter.

"You're going to make it. Just hang on, hang on," she whispered to the girl.

Outside she could hear loud running in the hallway. She yelled to the police officers who were moving through the building.

"In here! We're in here!"

Epilogue

26th and California Courthouse
July 18
2:43 P.M.

Janna rose from her chair, smoothing her navy skirt out before she addressed the jury.

"Ladies and gentlemen of the jury. You have heard the State's evidence. They have failed to meet their burden. They have failed to prove my client guilty beyond a reasonable doubt. I don't think that any one of you, in good conscience, can come out of your deliberation with all doubt removed that my client committed these crimes."

Janna cleared her throat and straightened her back, standing tall before the men and women seated in the jury box.

"I'm not going to waste your time pointing out all the holes in the State's case, the fact that they have not one eyewitness, no tangible evidence, and nothing was even found on my client.

"No ladies and gentlemen, I trust you to do the right thing in the burglary charge. What I want you to keep in mind is not that James Johannis allegedly stole a toilet from an empty building. Mind you, this is basically a victimless crime. But no, what I want you to keep in mind is the State's ridiculous charge of attempted escape against this man.

"The State would have you believe that James Johannis jumped out that window because he was guilty of stealing that toilet.

"But you heard from my client yourselves. He wasn't afraid to get up there and tell you what happened, not only on the night the toilet was stolen, but also on the day he jumped out the courthouse window.

"James Johannis feared for his life, ladies and gentlemen, and for good reason. He had discovered a doctor working in the jail was committing unspeakable acts. His help provided authorities with the evidence, the facts they needed to piece a complex puzzle together. Based on his help, a prominent young woman was rescued from sure death. And is he rewarded for that? No. Instead he stands trial here today, accused of stealing a toilet.

"And where is the doctor? Did he come forward to declare his innocence, to refute any of James's claims? No. The doctor is gone. Disappeared. Still at large.

"Ladies and gentlemen, we have the wrong man in custody. We're looking the wrong way. The real evil is Dr. Mason Von Patton. With his sick and twisted personal agenda, the doctor was allowing inmates to go untreated for serious illnesses. He was watching them die of AIDS. And for what? So he could say he earmarked the newest and latest HIV strand, a strand that moved in more quickly than any previous strand. All so he could obtain more funding for his lab. And James knew. It was this horrid doctor who caused my client to flee, to run for his life. James Johannis justifiably believed no one would take his word over a reputable doctor's. He would have been sentenced to death, waiting in his cell for whenever Dr. Von Patton decided to finish him off.

"James Johannis had no options. His fate was determined by his circumstances, circumstances dictated by this society. James had to take matters into his own hands as a matter of survival.

"I ask you to keep that in mind when you render your verdict this afternoon, or tomorrow morning, or whenever it is that you've reached your final determination. Thank you for your time and patience."

Janna returned to the defendant's table and sat back down next to James Johannis, winking at him.

"I feel good about this," she whispered.

"I hope so," he said.

"We'll just have to wait and see what they do."

"Okay then, we wait."

James put his head down on the table, wondering

what verdict the jury would bring back and when. Janna looked back at Jack Stone, who was standing at the rear of the courtroom and he smiled at her. She smiled back.

ABDUCTED

BRIAN PINKERTON

Just a second. That was all it took. In that second Anita Sherwood sees the face of the young boy in the window of the bus as it stops at the curb—and she knows it is her son. The son who had been kidnapped two years before. The son who had never been found and who had been declared legally dead.

But now her son is alive. Anita knows it in her heart. She is certain that the boy is her son, but how can she get anyone to believe her? She'd given the police leads before that ended up going nowhere, so they're not exactly eager to waste much time on another dead end on a dead case. It's going to be up to Anita, and she'll stop at nothing to get her son back.

BODY PARTS
VICKI STIEFEL

They call it the Grief Shop. It's the Office of the Chief Medical Examiner for Massachusetts, and Tally Whyte is the director of its Grief Assistance Program. She lives with death every day, counseling families of homicide victims. But now death is striking close to home. In fact, the next death Tally deals with may be her own.

Boston is in the grip of a serial killer known as the Harvester, due to his fondness for keeping bloody souvenirs of his victims. But many of those victims are people that Tally knew, through her work or as friends. Tally realizes there's a connection, a link that only she can find. But she'd better find it fast. The Harvester is getting closer.

THE
CRIMINALIST
WILLIAM RELLING JR.

Detective Rachel Siegel is a twelve-year veteran of the San Patricio Sheriff's Department. But she's never seen anything like the handiwork of the Pied Piper, the vicious serial killer who's been terrifying that part of California for months. Because she's the best at what she does, it's now her job to catch this maniac—but she has very personal reasons, too, for wanting him stopped

Kenneth Bennett works for the Department of Neuropsychiatry at St. Louis's Washington University. There's something special about the Pied Piper case that draws Bennett almost against his will to the west coast. He has no choice but to help Siegel in her frantic search—even if it gets both of them killed in the process.

ANDREW HARPER

RED ANGEL

The Darden State Hospital for the Criminally Insane holds hundreds of dangerous criminals. Trey Campbell works in the psych wing of Ward D, home to the most violent murderers, where he finds a young man who is in communication with a serial killer who has just begun terrorizing Southern California—a killer known only as the Red Angel.

Campbell has 24 hours to find the Red Angel and face the terror at the heart of a human monster. To do so, he must trust the only one who can provide information—Michael Scoleri, a psychotic murderer himself, who may be the only link to the elusive and cunning Red Angel. Will it take a killer to catch a killer?

Dorchester Publishing Co., Inc.
P.O. Box 6640
Wayne, PA 19087-8640

_____5275-X
$6.99 US/$8.99 CAN

Name: _____

Address: _____

City: _____ State: _____ Zip: _____

E-mail: _____

I have enclosed $_____ in payment for the checked book(s).

For more information on these books, check out our website at www.dorchesterpub.com.
_____ *Please send me a free catalog.*

EAST OF THE ARCH

ROBERT J. RANDISI

Joe Keough's new job as "Top Cop" for the mayor of St. Louis has him involved in more political functions than investigations. But all that changes when the bodies of pregnant women are discovered on the Illinois side of the Mississippi. Suddenly Keough finds himself on the trail of a serial killer more grotesque than anything he's seen before.

When the offer to join a special statewide serial killer squad comes his way, Keough has to make a decision that could change his personal and professional life forever. But through it all he continues to work frantically, battling the clock to find the perpetrator of these crimes before another young woman and her unborn baby are killed.

ISOLATION
CHRISTOPHER BELTON

It was specially designed to kill. It's a biologically engineered bacterium that at its onset produces symptoms similar to the flu. But this is no flu. This bacterium spreads a form of meningitis that is particularly contagious—and over 80% fatal within four days. Now the disease is spreading like wildfire. There is no known cure. Only death.

Peter Bryant is an American working at the Tokyo-based pharmaceutical company that developed the deadly bacterium. Bryant becomes caught between two governments and enmeshed in a web of secrecy and murder. With the Japanese government teetering on the brink of collapse and the lives of millions hanging in the balance, only Bryant can uncover the truth. But can he do it in time?

Dorchester Publishing Co., Inc.
P.O. Box 6640
Wayne, PA 19087-8640

5295-4
$6.99 US/$8.99 CAN

Please add $2.50 for shipping and handling for the first book and $.75 for each additional book. NY and PA residents, add appropriate sales tax. No cash, stamps, or CODs. Canadian orders require $2.00 for shipping and handling and must be paid in U.S. dollars. Prices and availability subject to change. Payment must accompany all orders.

Name: _____

Address: _____

City: _____ State: _____ Zip: _____

E-mail: _____

I have enclosed $_____ in payment for the checked book(s).

For more information on these books, check out our website at www.dorchesterpub.com.
_____ *Please send me a free catalog.*